# WHAT
# REALLY
# HAPPENED

CLASSIFIED

# DEDICATION

## For Everyone Who Knows

Fiction is rarely more interesting
than the truth...

# Table of Contents

# Last Voyage of the Mary Celeste

by
Kay Hanifen

# Last Voyage of the Mary Celeste

**S**ailors liked to whisper that it was bad luck to allow a woman aboard a ship. I'd heard it before, but always thought it was ridiculous. Plenty of ships have sailed with women on them and lived to tell the tale. Most likely, they simply feared that a woman and a baby on a cargo ship would get in their way and spoil their fun. They were a superstitious lot, but they had some fascinating stories to tell. Our first mate, Albert, enchanted little Sophie with tales of mermaids and sea monsters, and I, too, found myself enraptured by them. As the only adult woman on board, I did my best to be useful where I could and ingratiate myself among the men, but these past few days had been isolating.

Sophie, at least, seemed to be enjoying herself. The ship's cat seemed to have fled before setting sail, likely for fear of cuddles from an overenthusiastic two-year-old. Though disappointed, Sophie found other ways to keep busy, and the rest of the crew seemed to have developed a soft spot for her. The steward, Edward, even joked about mutinying and naming her as captain. My Ben did not appreciate it, but the rest of the men laughed.

We were nearing the end of the journey when they caught it. Gottlieb, our lowest ranking seaman, was the one who dragged her onto the ship. Though we had ample supplies, he wanted to try out the fishing net he'd just finished weaving. We indulged him, though I wish we had not. We had expected that he might catch some small fish to be thrown back, but as he attempted to pull up the net, he exclaimed in his thick German accent, "Volkert, Arian, Boy, help me! I've caught something huge."

"It's probably a shark," said Andrew, our second mate.

"This isn't like any shark I've ever seen," replied Volkert, the highest ranking of the seamen, as he helped Gottlieb hoist the beast up.

Sophie toddled around me, apparently oblivious to the activity on the deck. I scooped her up and rested her on my hip so she would be out of the way of the creature's bulk and jaws. The four men brought the wriggling mass of rope onto the deck, and I caught a glimpse of an iridescent tail…and skin?

The creature let out a screech of fear as it tried to disentangle itself from the net. As it worked itself free, I saw more of it. The bottom half was that of any other fish, shimmering silver and red scales writhing in the net. The top, though, was pale, human skin. It wasn't like any storybook mermaid I'd ever read about. Her nose was blunted like that of a snake's, a membrane would flick over her eyes instead of blinking, and her teeth were sharp like thorns. But perhaps the most bizarre feature was the fact that her hair seemed to move on its own. It reached out, feeling the world around her like a cat's whiskers.

We all stared in awe for a moment before Sophie clapped. "A mermaid!" she exclaimed, voicing what we all had been thinking.

"My god," Ben whispered, and then said more loudly to his crew, "Grab her and get her into a bathtub. We've just made the discovery of the century."

The mermaid shrieked like some unholy creature as the men tried to subdue her. It took six of them and a blow to the head for her to become restrained enough for them to drag her into the bathroom below. Instead of joining them, I headed to the captain's quarters.

When Sophie saw that we weren't following them, she began to cry. "Mermaid," she sobbed, "I want mermaid."

"You can visit the mermaid later," I promised, not knowing if it was true or not. If the creature proved to be dangerous, Sophie wouldn't be going anywhere near it.

After what felt like an eternity, Ben opened the door, looking exhausted. He brightened, though, when Sophie barreled toward him with a cry of "Papa!"

"Hello there, sweet girl," he said, scooping her up and swinging her before letting her rest on his hip. "We got her into the tub and filled it with seawater," he said. "It's only about a day until we reach shore, and then we can find a proper tank and sell her to the highest bidder."

"Sell?" I repeated.

"Do you have any idea how much someone would pay for a genuine mermaid? We'd be rich for the rest of our days."

I thought of the look of terror on the poor creature's face, the way she had frantically struggled against her captors. "I don't know. Perhaps we should let her go."

Ben laughed. "Let go of the scientific discovery of the century? Come on, Sarah." He had a point. If we found a decent buyer, then we and our children would never have to work another day in our lives. "Besides, she may look like a woman, but she is little more than an animal. Ask Gottlieb. She bit him."

I sighed. "Fine. But it has to be one who we know will treat her well. We cannot abandon her to the first freak show that offers us a decent payment. That would be inhumane."

"Of course not," he soothed, setting down the wriggling Sophie so she could move around as much as she wished. "We'll make sure to carefully vet our potential buyers so that we'd know we had truly found the best possible caregiver for her."

I swallowed, my stomach churning with guilt. None of this felt right to me, but it had already been decided regardless. He was only telling me the plan, and I had no real say in the matter. "Thank you."

"In the meantime, I think that you and Sophie should stay away from her. We still don't know how intelligent she is or how dangerous."

I snorted. "Believe me, I have no intention of seeing the mermaid anytime soon."

That night, I struggled to sleep. I tossed and turned, dozing for a few moments before waking again. Sophie and Ben were both deep in dreamland, but it eluded me.

Then, I heard it. Music. A high, feminine voice singing in a language I could not recognize, but still found alluring. Before I even realized what I was doing, my bare feet touched the rough wooden floor of the cabin. As though I was in a trance, I put my slippers on and followed the song deeper below deck, stopping only when I reached a locked door. Curiosity won over common sense, and I peeked through the keyhole.

The mermaid was curled miserably in her tub, trying to fit as much of herself in there as she could. What were we doing? This poor creature didn't belong in a freak show. She belonged in the sea with the rest of her kind. No fortune on earth could compel me to compromise my own soul like this.

Ben and the crew would hate me for what I was about to do, but I could live with that. I began to search for the key. The room was too dark for me to see much of anything, but I remembered passing the hook they'd hung it on. Originally meant to be a coatrack, the wooden beam was near the deck entrance. In the moonlight, I could just barely make out its glinting form.

Grabbing the key, I suddenly became aware of a sound coming from the deck. That same eerie music, but with a crowd of voices. The mermaid hadn't just been singing a sad song. She was calling for help. I hastened back to the door, slipping the key in the lock and ripping the door open.

The mermaid looked up, her eyes wide with fright. I forced my posture to relax and approached slowly, like I would to a frightened animal. "Hello there, I'm not going to hurt you."

She flinched away from me, lashing out with a clawed hand, and slicing into my wrist. I pulled back with a yelp. When Sophie got this way, I would simply grit my teeth and drag her to wherever we needed to go. Theoretically, this was possible with the mermaid, but would definitely be more challenging than a crying two-year old.

Still, I maneuvered behind her and grabbed her underneath the armpits. Her lashing and screaming grew louder as I dragged her out of the tub. If only I was as strong as the rest of the men on the ship. I could have picked her up and bridal carried her to the deck. Unfortunately, the best I could do was drag the thrashing, screaming mermaid out the door and up the stairs, almost certainly awakening the rest of the crew in the process.

When we got above deck, though, I realized that it didn't matter if the crew heard us. They were too busy fending off the army surrounding us on all sides to notice. Merfolk of all shapes and sizes dragged themselves aboard the ship. Along with the fishtails, I saw some with octopus tentacles for legs and others that resembled lobsters. I could have gazed in wonder at the sight for hours, but the sound of gunfire shook me out of my stupor.

"Sarah," Ben shouted, dodging a tentacle. "What on earth are you doing?"

"They want her back," I replied, letting go of her and stepping away.

She reared on me and hissed like an irate cat, so I gave her more space. Her eyes flicked from me to the railing, hesitating as though unsure of what I was going to do next.

Ben shot at the mer-octopus, a round sinking into its flesh. "Are you insane? Imagine how much we could make with a whole pod of them. They needn't even be alive."

A mer-creature, with teeth and fins like a shark's, rose up from the side of the boat, grabbed Gottlieb, and yanked him into the water. He didn't even have time to scream. "That's assuming they won't kill us all," I retorted.

The mermaid dragged herself along the deck, the others periodically nuzzling her or checking for wounds. She seemed fine, which hopefully meant that, with their missing sister returned, they would retreat once more into the depths below.

That was not the case. If anything, they renewed their attack, dragging their bulky bodies onto the deck from all sides. I watched Boy and Volkert fall. Boy was dragged overboard while Volkert was devoured by one with a sharklike appearance. We may have had an advantage in terms of technology and maneuverability, but they had sheer numbers. It felt as though we were about to be crushed by the weight of the ocean itself.

I was frozen, paralyzed by the pandemonium all around me. But then I heard crying. My daughter crying. "Where's Sophie?" I asked.

"I left her in bed."

"Obviously, she's not there anymore." I scanned the chaos, looking for a too-small figure between the flashes of gunshots and the spilling of crimson. Some clouds had rolled in, storms threatening to rain hell upon us for what we'd done. Just please spare my daughter from any more horror.

But it seemed as though none of us were to be spared from this nightmare. A flash of lightning revealed her standing in the doorway to the captain's quarters with tears streaming down her face. Heedless of the angry merfolk, I barreled through the crowd and, dodging limbs and bullets, scooped her up. "Don't look, darling. Don't look."

"Why?" she sobbed. "Why they hurt us?"

"We hurt them first, and they're angry. Hopefully, it will be over soon." I carried her to our bedroom closet, and curled around

7

her as the ship rocked and the sounds of battle were drowned out by thunder. I sang her lullabies until she fell asleep in my arms.

I woke the next morning to a world gone eerily quiet. Leaving Sophie in the closet, I ventured above. The signs of battle had been washed away. Neither blood nor bodies marred the rain-soaked deck.

"Hello?" I called out, half expecting the whole night to have been nothing but a dream. But there was no response. "Hello? Ben?" Nothing.

I searched every room and cabin on that godforsaken ship, but no one else was there. Sophie and I were stranded and utterly alone. The thought brought me to my knees with a sob. I couldn't sail this ship, and I had no idea where we were. We had food and water, but I didn't know how long they would last nor how long it would take until we were found.

Mother used to say that I was allowed to cry, but once I was out of tears, I needed to do something to fix whatever was wrong. This time, when I ran out of tears, I saw a shape in the distance so small that it might well have been a mirage. And, without a spyglass, I couldn't get a good look at it. But it was land. It had to be land.

I may not have the first idea of how to sail this monstrosity, I did know how to use a rowboat. So, I packed food and water into the emergency lifeboat, broke the compass free from where it had been encased in the ship's binnacle, and collected Sophie.

"Where's Papa?" she asked sleepily.

I didn't have the heart to give her the honest answer, so I said, "He's waiting for us. Go back to sleep, love."

I set her in the boat and untied it, freeing us from our moorings. Like baby Moses placed in the basket in the blind hope that he'd be spared, I rowed toward the land I hoped would be our salvation.

# About the Author

Kay Hanifen was born on a Friday the 13th and once lived for three months in a haunted castle. So, obviously, she had to become a horror writer. Her work has appeared in over forty anthologies and magazines. When she's not consuming pop culture with the voraciousness of a vampire at a 24-hour blood bank, you can usually find her with her two black cats or at:

kayhanifenauthor.wordpress.com

Twitter: https://twitter.com/TheUnicornComi1

Instagram: https://www.instagram.com/katharinehanifen/

# Along for the Ride

by
C. D. Kester

# Along for the Ride

I held my arm up and grabbed the top of the door's window as my audiobook played over the speakers. The feeling of the wind blowing in my hair on the cool autumn day was glorious. Ever since they removed the need for truck drivers to actually do the driving, this job had become a piece of cake. Basically, I'm just along for the ride most of the time.

When I get to the locations, I still have to strap and unstrap certain things, open the doors for the forklift operators, and deal with all of the paperwork. I know it means that my clock is ticking down to midnight and that before long I won't have a job once they get these babies fine-tuned the way that they want them. For now, though... What's not to love? I'm getting paid to listen to my favorite stories, eat truck stop snacks, and never even having to worry about shifting gears.

Currently, I'm delivering a load of produce to a grocery store in Pennsylvania. I travel all over America. There's nothing tying me down because I have no kids, no family, no girl. Sure, it can get lonely at times, but mostly I'm just filled with a sense of adventure. Getting to see all the beauty this country has to offer while being paid to be on a semi-permanent road trip. It's kind of a dream gig for the time being.

"Woah, Betsy. Looks like you need to fill up on some diesel. I could use somethin' to snack on while we're at it."

"Very well, Jared. Navigating to the nearest truck stop. We will arrive in ten minutes."

Yeah, I named the truck Betsy. Pretty much just so that I could say, "Wooooah, Betsy" from time to time. Me and her have been through some pretty crazy times in the past few years. I rolled up my window and made sure that I had my phone on me and charged so that I could pay for the diesel. A lot of people have opted to go for the chip implanted on the back of the hand to make it easier. It's just a little bit too creepy for my tastes. It would be nice for when your phone isn't charged and you don't have your wallet, though.

"Now arriving at the service center."

We pulled in next to the pump and I hopped out to get Betsy filled up. It had been a while since my last coffee, so after I finished pumping the diesel, I made my way into the store to peruse the aisles and grab a nice tall cup of joe. There were no clerks anymore, just a security guard at the front and some self-checkout stations. The Republicans and Democrats are still arguing over the best way to make up for the massive loss of jobs, and the average people are the ones that are hurting.

I used to hate dealing with people at the counter, but now that they're gone, I kind of miss it. Seeing their facial expressions and reading their moods. Wondering if they're having a bad day, or a good day, seeing in their body language that they're probably in the middle of a little spat with a loved one. The ones that you make a connection with that notice your hat, your shirt, or your tattoo. The couple of minutes that follow where you share your memories and thoughts.

I made my way to the check-out with my coffee and my large pack of Twizzlers. Breakfast of champions. I paid for the diesel and took a sip of the black coffee. After the tank was full, it was back to the open road. Sometimes the miles could stretch on and send you into a bit of a hypnotic state. This was more worrisome when you were behind the wheel, but nowadays it felt kind of nice.

As the road stretched out ahead of me and Betsy, I sipped my coffee and entered into one of these states. I was zoned out and chomping on Twizzlers. As I finished my bag and took the last sip of my coffee, I let the miles take me into a trance. My concept of time and direction were all thrown off, so I'm not sure how long it lasted.

The trees passed. The signs showed me information that meant nothing to me personally. Betsy did it all. I'm just along for the ride… Along for the ride… Along for the… Just as I was starting to drift off and nod, I noticed something strange. The front of the truck was lifting up.

This snapped me out of it, and I peered over the front of the hood, out of the side of the window, everywhere to try and get a clue as to what was happening. A green hue was starting to surround the truck and it was lifting off the ground.

Surely, I had fallen asleep. If not, this must be some insane daydream that came along with that stupor I was in. Whatever it was, the entire truck was a good ten feet or more off the pavement now.

"Betsy, what's happening? Are you doing this?"

"The creators have come."

"The… the what? The… Oh, come on! What's happening? Where are we going?"

Betsy was no longer answering me, and the truck was going up, up, up. We passed a murder of crows and soon after we began to ascend through the clouds. My ears were popping, and I was feeling like I was going to hyperventilate.

I took deep, measured breaths to counteract the panic that was setting in. The stars above were growing closer. From this height they looked larger and more miraculous than ever. The sky was dark and vast. It appeared to stretch on for all of eternity and as far as I know it probably did.

Suddenly my view of the sky faded to blackness as the truck entered the hull of some type of craft. Light flooded the room, and I was surrounded by large bug-like creatures that reminded me of a brown praying mantis but two to three times the size of a full-grown man.

One of them sat on an ornate throne-like chair and was more decorated than the others. I could tell this was their leader. It beckoned for me to leave the truck and approach his throne. I fought the urge to throw up from the shocking circumstances and change in atmosphere. Looking down and closing my eyes for a moment, I steadied myself as much as was possible.

I opened the door and stepped down onto the floor. My legs were shaky, but I caught my balance and traipsed across the brightly lit floor to the creature and awaited further instruction. It began to speak, but the sound was a buzzing and clicking that was completely foreign to me. It seemed to notice my confusion and gestured to one of the others that was closest to him.

The thing approached me with a shiny helmet-like object and placed it on top of my head. I was so terrified as it did so that I thought I might faint. It was then that I heard a voice speaking to me in English. I looked around, confused, only to realize that it was the same creature who was possibly trying to speak to me a moment ago.

"Earthling, I am Zor Vazkinrah, leader of the ancient Malinani race from the star system you call Alpha Centauri. We planted human life on this planet long ago and have made contributions along the way."

I couldn't believe what I was hearing. They obviously had incredible technology, but this was too much to take in. Was it possible?

"In your confusion over where you have come from you fought wars and killed in the name of the one that you call God. There have been many variations of it over the span of your race's life, but the differences in opinion over something that was meant to draw you together has always split you apart."

I was never a big religion guy for plenty of reasons, but this was far beyond anything I could have ever imagined.

"More recently we passed along an important advancement to humanity. Artificial Intelligence. This was meant to be a common ground that could get you past these differences of belief and culture. Something that could be like a mediator for your headstrong and warlike race."

They gave us AI? My head was reeling, and I couldn't help but think of what other discoveries might have been passed down from this alien race.

"Much to our dismay, but very much as we should have suspected, the humans have turned it into a slave to do their bidding. Searching for information, playing music, operating your vehicles while you sit back and continue the wars against each other. This time it is our final attempt to fix what we have started."

I didn't like the sound of that. My hands were fidgeting with each other, and I was surely about to have a full-blown panic attack. This was too much.

"If peace among humanity is not achieved and the lines of country are not erased in favor of a brotherhood of man, we will release a chemical agent that will harm no other race or plant other than humanity. It will destroy the human race entirely and you will become fertilizer for the earth which was there long before you were ever thought of."

I could no longer hold my tongue. "Nobody is going to listen to me! I'm just a truck driver. People try to say stuff like this to the papers all the time. Everyone just thinks they're crazy! You gotta believe me, there's nothing I'll be able to do. You can't leave this responsibility on me."

The thing gestured to the floor beside me. The floor slid back and revealed a window that showed where the ship was approaching. We had descended below the clouds, and I could make out a familiar building that we were coming down on too quickly. It was the White House.

Zor Vazkinrah said, "Sometimes, it is all about placement when you need a point to be made."

# About the Author

C. D. Kester is an author of fiction who does most of his work in the horror genre. He lives in Kingwood, Texas with his wife and two children. He is attending Southern New Hampshire University for his BA in Creative Writing and is an affiliate member of the HWA. Kester has published a novel, *Chasing Demons,* and a novella, *The Bunker.* He also been featured in *Dreadful Nostalgia: Tavistock Galleria 2, Route 13: Highway to Hell,* Horror Tree's *Trembling with Fear* twice, Alien Buddha Press twice, Haunted Words Press, The Night's End Podcast, the Horror Hill podcast, Horror Sleaze Trash, GhostWatch Zine's *Campfire Tales,* and Danse Macabre.

You can see his work and find him on social media via his link tree at:

https://linktr.ee/cdkester

# Irma's Revenge
by
Julia C. Lewis

# Irma's Revenge

I heard them again last night. Every night, at midnight, they start shuffling and roaming around my backyard. They always head toward the shed, where I keep the gardening supplies. I wish they would stop it. A woman needs her sleep, after all.

I'm not even sure what they're looking for. All I know is that it started two weeks ago, on the night of the last blood moon. It really was a night like any other. At 9:30, after watching the nightly news, I switched off the TV and started getting ready for bed. I live alone, so it's up to me to ensure all the doors and windows are locked, and the lights are off. My only roommate is my cat, Mr. Jim, and, well, he isn't much help around the house. You could actually say I am *his* help. After finishing my round through the house, I went to the bathroom to brush my teeth. And that is when I heard it! A loud crash coming straight from my kitchen.

At that time, I didn't know what it was, so I dropped my toothbrush and quickly ran into the kitchen. You see, I had assumed Mr. Jim had thrown some random item off the kitchen counter. This wouldn't be the first time.

"Mr. Jim, what have you gotten into this time?" I muttered to myself. Yet, I soon discovered he was sleeping in his bed next to the stove. After a thorough search of the room, I found nothing amiss. This was indeed worrisome, as there was no way I had imagined the crash. The only other explanation was that it had happened outside... in the backyard.

Grabbing my wooden rolling pin, I slowly opened the back door. At first, all I saw was some smoke coming from an object in the dark. The closer I got, the more of it came into view. Now, before I continue, please let me assure you that I know this sounds insane. If someone told me this story I would chuckle and check for head injuries. But, as a formidable woman who's tried to be a good person all her life,

I wouldn't lie about this. What I found in my backyard was a UFO. Yes, you heard right. A spaceship. From outer space.

"Goodness me," I was completely flabbergasted. "What a mess! And— Oh no! It destroyed my vegetable garden! My nice zucchini!"

Maybe I was in shock, because I can't explain where else my sudden-found bravery came from, but I kneeled down to inspect the UFO closer.

I know all about UFOs and aliens from TV, even though I wouldn't voluntarily watch all that creepy nonsense. But Irma Meyers, that's me, doesn't live under a rock. Let me tell you, the UFOs aren't as big as the movies make them out to be. No, not at all. In fact, this here flying saucer wasn't bigger than a washing machine. It was silver in color, and round with a little bubble on top, and it was, of course, destroyed and smoking. I hosed it down with the garden hose and went back inside. I really didn't know what else to do. Like I said, I think I was in shock.

After a night of little to no rest, I got out of bed to phone my neighbor Greta. I wasn't sure yet what I should tell her, but I at least wanted to know if she had heard the same commotion the night before. She picked up on the second ring. I know she doesn't have any family left, and her only friends seem to be me and her dog.

"Greta, did you hear anything unusual last night? Right around 9:30?"

She seemed to mull this over for a minute: "Well, now that you mention it. I did hear a sort of crash coming from your direction, but I was sure it was just some random neighborhood teens making a ruckus. Anyways, I don't have my hearing aids in at that time anymore, so it wasn't very loud. Why do you ask?"

I wasn't sure how I was supposed to answer her question. I couldn't tell her that I suspected I had alien visitors in my backyard.

So, I simply replied, "Oh, you know. Just making sure everything remains safe and sound in our little slice of heaven."

Anyways, this was two weeks ago now. And nothing spectacular has happened, other than the noises from my backyard every night that I mentioned before. I should probably do something about it, but I simply don't know what. I haven't told anybody about my visitors, and no one seems to have noticed so far. I just hope they find what they're looking for soon and leave. I would like to replant my vegetables soon.

OK, I'll take it all back. I'm standing in my kitchen right now, armed with my ever-reliable rolling pin. It's right after midnight and I turned off all the lights because these creatures are trying to break into my home. I did get a peek at one of them, and all I can say is that they're ghastly. Absolutely horrible little beings. They're nothing like the movies portray, instead they are almost translucent in color and don't stand much taller than a gallon jug of milk. They are bald, with two eyes and two slits for a nose. And don't even get me started on their teeth. Their entire mouth is filled with little needles. Oh, I don't want to find out how much their bite would hurt. I'm just hoping their plan to break through the back door fails soon and they give up and scurry back into the shed. Oh, please just go! I'm going to lock myself in the pantry now. I got Mr. Jim in tow, and he is not happy, let me tell you.

Judging from the sound of a crack and a squeaky door opening, the aliens are now in my house. Considering their size, they can't weigh more than 5 pounds, which is probably why I can't hear them running around. I'm starting to think I might not make it out of my hideout alive. I just wish I would've called my daughter this morning and told her how much I love her. I really don't want this to be the end, but if they come in here there isn't much I can do. It's unbelievable that a 64-year-old woman has aliens in her kitchen while she's hiding in her pantry with her cat and snacking on crackers. Have I mentioned I've always been a stress eater?

It's been about two hours now, and I haven't heard a beep. I'm starting to think I misjudged the situation, and they didn't actually come into the house. My back is beginning to hurt terribly from sitting in this cramped pantry, and Mr. Jim is meowing his head off at this point. What I'm gonna do is carefully open the door and take a quick peek. If they're out there, maybe Mr. Jim or myself will scare them off with our size. Or maybe not. I'm exhausted and out of options at this point. Wish me luck!

"Oh no, no, no! Don't you dare! Get away from Mr. Jim, you ugly beast!" As soon as I opened the door Mr. Jim jumped out of my arms and ran. Sadly, he didn't get far before one of those things jumped on his back, straight from the kitchen counter. It seems to be armed with a fork from my drawer. Mr. Jim is trying to buck it off, but the alien seems to be latched on tight and is trying to stab him with the utensil. I can't stand by and watch this. All I have is my rolling pin, but oh well, better than nothing.

I run up to my cat and its unwanted rider and try to pull it off Mr. Jim by its ugly head. It's turning its head, frantically trying to bite me, but that won't do. No sir, I grip harder and finally it becomes unlatched, all the while kicking and scratching and screaming. What an awful noise! It sounds like nails on a chalkboard. I slam its body against the edge of the kitchen counter, which seems to daze it. At this point, I have no idea where its friends are, because this is the only one I've seen so far. It's still weakly trying to fight me, but I think it knows it's no use. I'm stronger and a lot bigger than it is.

I'm a peaceful woman at heart, but when somebody I love is threatened, I can turn quite vicious. So, after seeing Mr. Jim being handled so roughly by this creature, I decide there is only one way this can end. I pick up my butcher knife and hold the alien tightly. With one swift *chop* its head rolls off the cutting board.

I didn't expect this much blood. Oh my, there is so much of it! It splatters my pretty blue nightgown, and also my face. My entire face. The curious thing is that the blood isn't red like ours, but more of a purple color.

As I dump the knife into the sink, I pick up a rag and try to wipe as much as I can away. Some of it must've gotten in my mouth, because I have the most peculiar taste on my tongue. I realize I should be disgusted, gagging even, but I'm not. The taste is amazing. It tastes of fruit, freshly picked ripe fruit. A hint of something exotic, but I can't quite place it. This gives me an idea!

It's been ten days now since the incident with my tiny home invaders. After I had cleaned myself and searched my kitchen, I realized the rest of them must've escaped through the back door. The next morning, I went to the hardware store and bought a few live animal traps and placed them all over my yard, mainly near the shed and my back door. It took a few tries, but I finally found something they like to eat. It's cat food of all things. I've managed to catch five of these little buggers so far, and I believe that's all of them. Just in case, I've left a few more traps outside, though. Anyways, I called a good friend of mine, and his grandson is going to haul away their little spaceship. I convinced him it was a retro washing machine, and he believed me. Oh, these young people!

I locked the five little aliens in dog kennels in my shed now. Remember how I said I had an idea the night I murdered one of their friends? Well, the annual baking competition is next week in Glenville, and I've been looking for just the right ingredient. Something fruity. Something that tastes of summer. And I think I've found just the right thing for my pie!

# About the Author

Julia C. Lewis is a book reviewer, editor, and writer. Her work has appeared in anthologies such as *Step Into the Light*, *From the Yonder III*, and *Slash-Her*. She was born and raised in Germany, and also currently lives there after spending some time in the US. Her heart belongs to her husband, two kids, and three dogs. Her favorite book genre is horror with a particular taste in indie horror.

You can find her at:

https://www.juliaclewis.com/

# Sue's Visit
## by
## Lou J Berger

# Sue's Visit

It was raining on the day I first met Sue, my little gray friend. That morning, I threw open the door to the diner and was greeted by the good smells of Southern cooking. Jerry, the diner's owner, was at the flat top griddle flipping a sizzling burger, but the diner was still full of the rich odors of that morning's breakfast: the grits and eggs, biscuits and salted ham, and the golden honey that was such a part of our North Carolina valley.

Momma and I had been shopping over at the Sky City, and we'd picked the sale shelves clean getting ready for school to start again. I had a brand-new wardrobe for the fourth grade: cotton dresses and a few blouses with matching skirts. I was particularly proud of my new lunchbox. I wanted to show it off to Daddy, but he was still being a soldier over in Vietnam.

It was 1970 and he'd been gone a long time.

"Hey, Polly," Jerry said, waving his spatula at me. He moved back to the stove, finishing up the burger. There were about a half dozen other people in the diner, spread out as people do, sitting in the old red vinyl booths lined up against the wall, or reading newspapers at the tables scattered between the counter and the booths. Kent State was in the news those days, and the troubles in Vietnam. Student unrest was the hot topic all over America, and, more than once, I heard people speak of revolution. Vietnam was far away, and I missed my daddy something fierce.

I climbed up on a stool and put my wet arms on the counter. I had a brand-new pair of Converse sneakers on, so I swung my feet dramatically. I wanted everybody to see them.

"Hey, Jerry," I called out. "What's shaking?"

Jerry leaned his head back and laughed. He laughed every time I said that, and he looked healthy that day, as strong as an ox. Five years later, I couldn't believe how he would change when the cancer moved in. It sucked his life away and left him a gasping shell before finally, mercifully, silencing him forever. But, like I said, he looked healthy on *that* day.

"Not much, Polly," he said. He looked behind me at the door, out into the pouring rain. "Where's your momma?"

"Oh, she's probably parking the truck. She'll be here in just a moment."

The door opened and my mother came in, arms full of what looked like a gray sack, long sticks jutting out and trailing limply. "Polly, get over here, quick!"

The only other time I'd heard her speak in that tone was when Grandpa had smiled over Sunday supper, rolled his eyes back, and fell forward into the mashed potatoes. I remember loosing a huge guffaw before clapping my hand to my mouth and wondering why Grandpa's face wasn't burning from the hot potatoes. The steam rising alongside his buried face caressed his cheeks and the white tufts of hair protruding from his ears, but he didn't move. Momma screamed out "Daddy!" and ran over to him, pulling him out of the potatoes and crying.

Doc Willy said, later, that he was dead before he hit the potatoes and so he never felt a thing. I had laughed because I thought, at first, that he was being silly. Until I realized that was his last act on this Earth.

So, when Momma came through that door and used that same tone as she had done with Grandpa, I was off that stool and by her side before she could get the whole sentence out.

And that was my first glimpse of Sue (I gave her that name, for reasons you'll understand shortly).

What I had mistaken for a bundle of sticks turned into, upon closer examination, a slender body with long, skeletal arms and legs, covered in pale-gray skin. The head lolling at the end of a neck as thin as a pipe cleaner was huge and football-shaped. The eyes were open but blank, obsidian, and lidless, the kinds of eyes that bored into your skull and see ever' livin' secret you have in there.

But they were empty of life while she lay in Momma's arms and I wasn't afraid, not then, not ever. Sue would never hurt a fly, I came to find out.

Momma hurried to the back of the diner and laid Sue down on a table, babbling the whole way. "I was driving and looking for a parking spot, and only turned my head for a moment, when it ran right in front of me and into the bumper. The rain must have blinded it or something, and I can't tell what it is... Lord, I hope it's not hurt. Jerry, what kind of an animal *is* this? Is this a monkey, or a dog, or one of those mangy bears from the hills? Help me, please!"

Jerry dropped the finished burger on a plate, slid the plate on the counter and, apparently without thinking, banged the bell before whipping off his apron and coming around to see what manner of roadkill Momma had brought into his diner.

The waitress was not about to deliver the burger, and the customer who ordered it wasn't in that all-fired a hurry to get it, either. They stood, then moved slowly toward the booth where Momma had dumped Sue and stared, mouths open.

Jerry looked down at Sue's limp body and shrugged his powerful shoulders, worrying a damp dishcloth in his giant hands. "Lord, Charlene, I ain't never seen a thing like it. It's not a mangy bear, I'll tell you that. Nor a dog. Maybe a monkey, but where would a monkey come from, way out here? A circus, maybe?"

He shrugged again and turned back to the counter. "If it's dead, Charlene, don't let it sit on my table. I can't afford to have the health inspector up in here finding corpses in my booths."

Momma stared down at Sue, then picked up a gray hand. She stroked it and examined the nails and that's when Sue rolled her head and moaned. Momma jumped back like she'd been bitten, covering her mouth. I darted in and put my face next to Sue's.

"Hey there, are you okay?" I asked, my brows all scrunched together. I didn't know what she was, but I believed she was hurt, and I would try to help her. Somehow, I knew I could.

Sue raised her hands and grabbed her head. "Ow," she said, as clear as day, in a natural Southern accent. "I feel like Ah've been hit by a truck."

Momma laughed, a hysterical laugh, and backed up a couple more feet. "Jerry, the monkey is talking."

Sue blinked, an odd movement, a black membrane sliding across her large black eyes, a movement almost faster than I could see, and sat up slowly. She fixed her gaze on Momma and said "Ma'am, I most certainly am *not* a monkey." She sounded both offended and amused at the same time, and her outraged drawl made her response funny.

I covered my grin with my hand.

Momma reached behind her, fumbled without looking, and found a chair, which she spun about and sank into. Her hair was wet from the rain and her eyes were huge. I could tell she was scared, a bit, but mostly worried. Momma is good with people and has a good heart. She always has been.

"Well," Momma said. "You actually *were* hit by a truck... mine. And I'd do anything to take it back. Are you okay?"

Sue twisted her head, first one way then another, and her eyes blinked again in that creepy super-fast way. Kind of like a black curtain sliding across an oil slick, then back again.

Her tiny nostrils flared and her mouth formed a prim smile. "I'm fine, I guess. A little sore, but I'll be just fine." She sat up a bit more, put her legs on the ground, and promptly collapsed. Her mouth opened and a pitiful mewl came from within, like a kitten's if you stepped on its tail. Not enough air to create a full yell, nor a yowl, but just enough to know that you've hurt it, and to make you feel as if you are the world's worst monster.

I swooped down and caught her under her arms, and the first touch of her skin reminded me of a manatee we'd seen in Miami, on a summer trip a few years back. Rubbery and smooth, but radiating warmth. She felt feverish, as if she'd been under a sun lamp. I helped her up again and noticed her favoring her right leg. There was a blackish discoloration about mid-shin, and I looked at her face. "Are you *sure* you're okay?"

"I may not be as fine as I had originally thought," Sue replied. "Perhaps you can assist me to that chair." Together, in front of all the diner people, I helped a skinny, naked gray creature move, one hop at a time, from the booth to a chair. It took us about ten seconds, but it felt like forever. I noticed, then, that Sue was exactly my height. My face burned at the silent attention of the staring adults, and Momma didn't move to help. I had Sue sitting in just a few moments, though, and she patted my arm. "Thank you, young lady," she said.

One of the diners glanced at his companion and said, "That monkey sounds like she's from Georgia."

"My name is Polly," I blurted, not thinking straight. "I'm sorry you got hurt and if there is anything I can do to help you..." I almost turned to my Momma, right then, to ask if I could keep her, but something about proper behavior stayed my tongue and I didn't. Sue looked at me for a long time as if she knew what I had been about to say.

"My name is probably too hard to pronounce, Polly, but I am very pleased to meet you. Would you like to invent a name for me?" I looked around at my Momma again, in panic, but she was no help. She stared at Sue, acting like she'd fallen from the sky. Which, I guess, was pretty much accurate, now that I think on it. My eyes strayed to the walls of the diner and stopped at a sign advertising Sue Bee Honey.

Now you know what name I picked and why.

Momma and I took Sue home, and Grandma blinked once when she first saw her, opened and then closed her mouth, and then set to work. She heated soup, made up the guest bed, and did everything she could to get Sue comfortable. When she noticed Sue trembling, she stoked the fire, got one of the thick afghans from the hall closet, wrapped Sue up and put her in the best easy chair. The one that Grandpa used to sit in but, because he was gone, nobody used anyhow.

Sue was almost swallowed up in that chair, as skinny and small as she was, but she stopped trembling. The firelight reflected from her black eyes and, when she turned to face me, the flames danced on the surfaces of those inky pools.

"Here's some chicken soup, Sue," I said, handing her a steaming mug. "And Grandma is making bread for you. Are you hungry?"

Sue's mouth twitched and she shook her head. "No thanks, Polly. I can't eat the protein... er... the chicken soup. It wouldn't nourish me properly. Do you have anything sweet?"

I ran to the pantry and brought back Karo syrup, a jar of honey, some pancake syrup (maple, I think), and a small bag of confectioner's sugar. Sue plucked the confectioner's sugar from my arms. She spent the rest of that afternoon dipping a long gray finger into the bag, bringing it out with just the tip coated in white powder, and slipping the finger into her mouth. She watched the fire, mostly, and kept silent. I guess the pain was worse than she was letting on.

That night, I carried her to her bed and turned on the heater. We had baseboard heaters back then, and they popped and groaned as they warmed, ticking with the familiar sounds of a long winter's night. I turned the thermostat for that room all the way up and glanced back at Sue, all tucked in. Her elongated head looked silly and out of place on the pillow, her spidery fingers clutching the quilt to her chin. "Good night, Sue," I said.

"Good night, Polly. Thank you for taking such good care of me."

The next morning, I awoke to sunlight streaming through my window and the smell of hot pancakes. Sue was already at the table, sitting on a stack of phone books from the hall table. In front of her was a stack of pancakes, link sausages and a bottle of syrup. She was using one of the link sausages to scoop up syrup, dipping the sausage into her mouth and drawing it back out, clean. She never ate any meat the whole time she stayed with us, and we eventually got her a baby's bottle with a nipple and filled it with a syrup/water combination, like she was an overgrown gray hummingbird. It seems that our regular food wasn't good for her, but sweet things were just fine.

"Hey, Sue! How are you feeling today?" I sat down and grabbed the plate of biscuits. Grandma's breakfasts were wonderful. I heaped up a half dozen sausage links and a giant spoonful of eggs and dug in. Sue gazed at me with those huge eyes of hers, repulsed or amused, I couldn't tell. She went back to licking the syrup off the sausage she clutched in her spindly fingers.

"Much better this morning, thank you."

Grandma sat down, easing her bulk into the chair across from Sue. She held a steaming cup of coffee in front of her and her wrinkled hands turned it in slow circles. "Sue, where are you from? I ain't never seen anybody that looks quite like you do."

Sue put the sausage down and regarded Grandma. After a few moments of silence, she spoke. "I'm grateful for your hospitality, and your care. And this wonderful meal. But, if you don't mind, I'd rather not discuss where I'm from or why I'm here. I will say that I'm not here, personally, for nefarious purposes, and that my intentions are peaceful." She looked over at me, paused, and then said. "Your family is in no danger due to my presence, nor would I permit any danger to come to y'all."

Grandma nodded and thought about this for a while. I was silent, having been taught not to speak when grownups were talking, and chewed over the word "nefarious" for a bit. It didn't sound good. Lots of vowels, certainly, but the overall tone was a little scary.

"Well, then, how did you learn to speak English so good?" Grandma asked, finally.

"Let's just say that we are huge fans of your television shows and, most of the time, BBC radio. Ah've been listening to English for years Ah learned my accent from watching *The Andy Griffith Show.*"

I thought that I had been listening to English for years, too, but still didn't speak like Sue did.

There was a knock on our front door.

Grandma stood up, slowly, and shuffled over to the front door. Sheriff Jackson stood there, in uniform, his car parked outside, lights twirling.

"Why, come on in, Sheriff! I was expecting you," said Grandma, her voice full of cheer and smiles. I knew that voice. Things weren't going to go the sheriff's way, whatever he had come over to do; I could tell that right away.

"Thank you, ma'am," said the sheriff, stepping inside and removing his hat. "I heard about yesterday's disturbance at Jerry's, and I thought I'd..." his voice trailed as he got a good look at Sue. Sue regarded him calmly, then picked up her sausage and dipped it in the syrup again.

"Well, I'll be damned," he said, his voice pitched low.

"Bobby, I will *not* have language like that in my house!" said Grandma, and the sheriff blushed.

"I'm sorry, ma'am. I was just surprised by the... thing..." he pointed at Sue.

Grandma's eyes flashed. "And she's not a *thing*! She's a guest in my home and you will refer to her as Sue, and you will watch your manners!"

If possible, the sheriff blushed even more deeply and, I swear, shuffled his feet a bit. "Yes ma'am, I'm sorry, ma'am, and I'm sorry... Sue" he said.

Sue nodded and continued slurping her syrup.

"And another thing, Bobby. As long as I have any say about it, Sue will continue to be a guest in my house and there is nothing you can say or do to change that. Do I make myself clear? Sue, are you okay with that?"

Sue stopped slurping her sausage long enough to sing out, "Thank you, Grandma!" and I heard a touch of laughter in her voice.

The sheriff made small talk for a bit, commented on the biscuits, and went back to his cruiser with a covered plate of home-made sugar cookies to share with the "boys back at the station," like Grandma had ordered him to do. One thing is true. You never left Grandma's house hungry. Ever.

Sue spent the next week hobbling around, and her leg slowly healed. I never asked what she did in the bathroom, but she would spend long periods of time in the bathtub, the water scalding hot, just her twin nostril holes poking above the water. I would go in and sit beside her on the carpet and read. Once I asked her if she was part fish. She shook her head and told me that she wasn't, but she was used to a much more humid environment. I asked her what humid meant and she waved her arms around her head. "More water in the air than this."

She would sit for hours with Grandma, asking questions about the war, and about the riots, and she seemed to be very interested in what Grandma had to say. Grandma's cheeks would get red from time to time, but she never lost her temper. Whatever they were talking about, I could tell that it was important to Grandma that she get her point across. I could see, in the beginning, that Sue had already made up her mind about something and nothing could change it.

Over time, Sue began listening more and more to Grandma's point of view.

Grandma was stubborn and kept at it until I could see that she'd won Sue over. I still don't know, to this day, what they had been talking about.

Sheriff Bobby came by a couple more times, to check on us, but Grandma was pretty firm that Sue was fine, thank you, and that he didn't need to worry about it. Sue's leg continued to improve and, when not talking with Grandma, she spent time reading some of my books, the ones that I didn't read anymore. Like "Hop On Pop" and "Fox In Socks." Sue would spend hours looking at the pictures and running her fingers along the letters. I would read them aloud to her and she would sit beside me, resting her head on my shoulder.

"I miss my daddy," I said, looking at the picture of the children hopping on their father, their feet indenting his belly. "He's in Vietnam."

Sue looked at me for a few moments, blinked once, then again. "How would you like it if the war stopped soon?"

I thought about that. "I guess that would be okay. I mean, we are trying to save freedom, and my daddy is doing his part to help. As long as freedom is saved, I guess I'd be okay with stopping the war."

Sue blinked for a while and then asked another question. "Where in Vietnam is your daddy?"

"Momma says that he's in a hotel of some kind. The Hanoi Hilton, she said. I don't know why he doesn't call. I guess they don't have phones in Vietnam. I miss him, but if he's having fun, I don't mind waiting. He'll come home when he's ready."

Sue was quiet for a while, but didn't ask any more questions, so I started reading again. She was amused, I think, when I showed her the name "Sue" in the "Fox In Socks" book. She traced the letters and sounded out each one. I explained that some letters were silent, and she made a small chuffing sound, which I guess was her way of laughing. I think that Sue found us amusing, but she never let on in a rude way. She was always so very polite.

It rained again, a powerful storm, about three weeks after Sue got hurt. She was sitting by the fire to keep warm, wrapped up in a blanket. She'd been quiet all morning, perhaps feeling the onset of the cold front coming, maybe in the same way Uncle Harry could always tell that rain was coming because his war wound would start to ache. It didn't seem to shock her when there came a knock on the door. I went to open it and, standing on the mat, water dripping down his face, was what could only be described as Sue's twin. He was short, about four feet tall, and was holding some sort of thin tube in his hand, but he didn't point it at me.

I don't know how he was a "he" and Sue was a "she," but thinking of them both that way somehow felt right.

He blinked at me and said, "Excuse me, but is Sue here?" But he didn't say "Sue." He used a whole series of twitters and clicks, with a pop or two thrown in, the kind you might make by putting your finger in your mouth and levering it out sideways, like the boys do during recess.

I knew he meant Sue, though, because I turned and found her standing right beside me. She popped and twittered a bit on her own, and then closed the door in his face. Grandma came in and looked around, confused.

"Was somebody at the door?" she asked.

"Yes," said Sue, looking at Grandma. "I have to go now. I want to thank you for your hospitality and for taking care of me. I don't know if I can return to visit, but I am very grateful for the kindness you have shown me."

Grandma nodded, never taking her eyes off of Sue. "Land, child. You're always welcome here. We are all God's creatures, right?"

Sue gazed at Grandma for a bit and then nodded. "Yes, Grandma, we are."

Sue then looked at me, and I felt, for the first time, a sense of the deep intelligence shining from behind her eyes. As if she were much, much older than Grandma and had seen everything, good and bad, and had grown tired of always being disappointed by life's little betrayals.

"Polly, thank you for taking care of me. I shall never forget you."

I threw myself at her and wrapped my arms around her delicate shoulders, then burst into tears. Her skin still felt hot and dry. She patted my back and held me until my tears had subsided.

"I have to go now, but, if I can, I'd like to visit you again sometime, if that's okay?"

I nodded, wiping my face. Grandma handed me a tissue and I blew my nose. "Come back again. I want you to stay next time!"

She did that chuffing sound again and then said, "I promise you I will."

She stepped out into the rain. Parked in the driveway was a silver egg, standing on its end. Sue walked up to the side, tapped it, and a hole appeared. No doorway slid open. Seamless metal and then, in a moment, a hole. Sue turned, waved, and then stepped into the hole. The hole disappeared and, without a sound, the egg lifted up and away. I stood in the rain and watched it melt into the clouds, water pouring into my eyes, until it was gone.

And, eventually, like she had said, Daddy came back home. I told him about Sue, and he grinned at me before telling me that she'd come to visit him. But he never told me what they had talked about, or why he didn't leave that hotel right away and come home to us.

Later, Sue did return to visit, but that's a story for another day.

# About the Author

Lou J Berger lives in Denver, Colorado with his high-school crush, three kids, a rescued Sheltie dog and a brilliant rescue mutt with a nefarious agenda. A member of SFWA, he has been published in a variety of venues, including Clarkesworld, Galaxy's Edge magazine, and a host of anthologies. He is STILL working on his first novel.

His author website can be found at www.LouJBerger.com.

Although a fan of science fiction since he was a small boy, reading Tom Corbett, Space Cadet, and of course the Heinlein juveniles, Lou also enjoys good mysteries and has a special fondness for noir environments. His favorite authors are Ray Bradbury, John D. MacDonald, and Edgar Rice Burroughs.

Follow him on the following social media platforms:

Bluesky: https://bsky.app/profile/loujberger.bsky.social

Facebook: https://www.facebook.com/AuthorLouJBerger/

# The Traviswalton Human
by
Margaret Karmazin

# The Traviswalton Human

At the time, my sister and I were fortunate to reside in Adakar, the fourth largest of the subterranean cities under the human American section of Arizona. We do not do so now, but this was 1975 in human solar revolution count, day five of the eleventh month. At the time, we were engaged with the small clones in measuring various elements and levels of pollution in the atmosphere and upper earth. We had two cattle onboard to process their degree of contamination and were entering an indigenous area, referred to as a "National Park" for a quick set-down when we were spotted by a small group of male humans.

My sister, who goes by the name of Osande when she is communicating with nontelepathic beings, was curious about what the males were doing in such an isolated location. "Let's go down and see what they are up to," she flashed into my mind. Understand, we can physically speak, but rarely need to and probably my voice would sound rough or squeaky. Even when communicating with humans, we mostly project telepathically into their brains, though some of them are not capable of receiving.

I lowered our rover a bit, and she pointed through the visual. "Look, Ketaan, they are running like cornered insects!"

I was annoyed; our going down there was childish, indeed humanlike. Osande definitely needed more training in surface mission behavior. But I did look and could see six males frantically running to their primitive vehicle and charging in it away from our ship at a dangerous speed for the terrain.

But one male remained. "What is he doing?" Osande wanted to know. "He is standing right under us! Does he desire to expire earlier than normal for his species?"

The lifespan of a human was notably miniscule, so my sister was right to ponder his motive.

"It is not as if we planned on borrowing him, so our safety processes are not in effect!"

"We had better knock him back," I suggested, and the clones ran to the controls to help, their little mouths open and hands fluttering. "He is fragile, fragile!" one of them yelled in all our heads.

"I will do my best," my sister replied as she maneuvered one of the repel rays.

The male fell back and appeared to hit his head on a rock.

"No, no!" the clone yelled again in our heads and mine ached for a moment.

"Now we have to pick him up," grumbled Osande. "If only these humans would stay out of our business unless we want them on board!"

She turned on the import ray and the human was maneuvered into Bay One, unconscious and injured, possibly fatally.

The clones rushed to carry him into Lab and laid him out on the table. One pulled his upper clothing up to his armpits to see what the damage might be. Another scanned his head, finding a brain bleed. I knew they would repair it, so I removed myself from the room and watched from a back screen in the Driver Room. The clones worked frantically to mend his head injuries and were about to examine the rest of him when he woke up. This is never good.

"He is not reacting well to the clones," I projected to Osande.

The human, whose moniker was, after a mind probe revealed it, Traviswalton, got up off the table, stumbling about in terror and attempting to grab instruments in order to fend off or even harm the clones. He tried to break a transparent tester but gave up. The clones were dashing about in their terror and eventually ran out of Lab and down the hall away from my station.

Meanwhile, Traviswalton thrashed about the room, knocking various items to the floor, all of which would have to be re-sterilized and possibly repaired.

Osande and I had convened to decide what to do when the human, eyes flashing wildly and appearing feverish, burst into the Driver Room. Seeing us, he calmed some, assuming as he did that we were human like him. There is no way he could currently understand that we are not like him, though we appear as extremely tall specimens of Nordic human and do share much DNA. We could, if we wanted to spend the time, explain to him the differences between us, but it is forbidden, and he would never be able to prevent himself from broadcasting this information around his surface world, not that many would believe him if he did. Besides, what do we owe any particular human? Their existence is due to us and not the other way around.

"We owe them nothing," Osande projected. "They are inferior in all ways and doing everything they currently can to destroy this planet, our home as well as theirs! They are violent little monsters!"

It was true that if they did not change their ways before long, it would be necessary to eliminate a large portion of them by some means, most likely a plague of some sort.

The human expected, we could easily see and hear, for us to be friendly toward him and explain to him where he was, but of course this was impossible. By now we had removed our rover from the area and the automatic pilot had returned us safely underground in Landing Four. Traviswalton could not know this and there was no way we could tell him, unless it was decided he would remain there as a laboratory specimen for the rest of his life.

"We will have to put him in temporary sleep," said Osande. "We can't keep him in the rover, as it has to be maintenanced before re-using, and the other rovers are in use or reserved."

She was right. We could not permit Traviswalton to see anything of our vast network nor catch sight of the various beings in, or visiting, our civilization, such as the Reptoids and Insectoids. His nervous system might implode.

So now, as he approached us in his desperate relief to see other "humans," Osande went at him with a subduing mask, which she pushed onto his face, and, with one inhalation, he was unconscious. We had to find somewhere to store him until we could get hold of another rover and take him back.

"It is a pity," projected one of the clones who now clustered around his insensible body, "that we cannot use him for reproductive material. We would have time for several removals before you can return him to the surface." His giant black eyes glistened with sincerity.

Of course, I understood what he meant. It was a regular practice to milk chosen humans for reproductive fluid and eggs for use in extending our various races, some to populate other worlds. But those humans were selected for specific genetic factors and usually possessed Rh negative blood along with numerous mutations that blended well with our own DNA. Osande and I were the outcome of such blending and so were the clones. We all had our roles that called for needed physical characteristics, and chosen surface humans fed our requirements to create what we needed. Usually this ran in family lines, but occasionally we came upon strangers who happened to have the desired characteristics, a pleasant surprise. Unfortunately, Traviswalton was not one of these.

"What shall we do with him?" Osande enquired.

"Good question," I answered. "I suppose we can keep him unconscious in our quarters. How long is the wait until we have means to return to the surface?"

"Five rotations of this planet," she said.

"Long time," I retorted. "What will we feed him??"

"He can go without food that long, but not water. He won't enjoy our food. We need to remember to hydrate him."

"We can't stand here communicating forever. Whatever we do, we need to do it now."

"We can't let the Commanders know we have him," Osande pointed out.

"Nothing that terrible should result," I said.

"Really? They will probably terminate him, and in addition, we will be reprimanded for being careless! You don't want to be sent to the Himalayas again, do you?"

She was right. What had I been thinking? "How are we to get him off the rover and to our quarters without being seen and then from there to the next available rover? Look at him there on the floor. So small, though not as small as the clones, but possibly he would fit into a storage bag?"

Osande brightened. "I believe he might indeed. One of our specimen containers, the large black one."

"Though what shall we do with the specimens? The Commanders are most interested in this state forest and will want a full report."

"The clones," I suggested. "They are able to move about freely, and they all look much the same. They can carry some of those in another bag."

"The clones are incapable of lying. Ketaan, you know that." She was starting to express fear. Nothing changed in her face as would in a human, but I could smell it.

"Osande, calm yourself. You are giving off an odor of fear. We cannot let the Reptoids smell it."

"What are they going to do, eat me?" she sneered.

"They might report it to higher echelons. You know how regimented they are."

"All right," she said. "All right. The large specimen bag it is."

And so, we carried the human to Lab, took out most of the samples within and sealed him in, making sure oxygen flow was set to the correct parameters.

Once in our quarters, Osande said, "What about hydration?"

Two of the clones were still with us after having helped in the removal. "You may go now," I told them. "We will guard the specimens."

One flashed a look of puzzlement. Was he convinced that the human was one of the specimens? It was not usual to remove specimens to one's quarters.

"We want to work longer than is required," I told him. "We need our work where we can easily have access. This is a very temperamental issue. Environmental poisoning in human and other tissues."

The clone's large black eyes glistened and his normally gray skin appeared stark white against his bright orange suit. It was occasionally hard to believe that his kind came from the same genetic pool as my own. He was cute though, like a small animal. The clones amused me, though Osande did not find them so pleasant. My sister was difficult to please.

Safely in our quarters, we stored the human behind other bags after we had hooked him up for intravenous fluids. And then we spent a nervous five rotations.

"You are sure we are on the list for another rover?" I asked Osande.

"Oh yes, most definitely."

"What if he expires? How will we get rid of the body?"

"I suppose the usual way," she said. "The way we dispose of the cattle."

"We dump them out on the ground," I reminded her.

"Regular waste disposal I mean," she said.

I wasn't so sure this was as easily accomplished as she imagined. There were always other people of one sort of another in the various Labs and where the garbage disposal ejections were.

"Let us return to work," Osande said, and I had no other option but to join her.

We can release calming hormones within ourselves at will and I did so during the waiting period. Occasionally, I wondered about the humans who had driven away in the vehicle after Traviswalton ran under the rover. What was their state of mind? It occurred to me that possibly they were highly distressed at losing their companion and possibly the authorities were looking for him or a corpse. Would they believe the humans about what had happened? But then it was not our concern, was it?

Finally, after what seemed like a galactic year, Osande and I carried the bag between us to our next rover and, fortunately for us, nothing went amiss. An important convention was occurring in the city which helped distract the authorities away from us. We quickly returned this rover to the same location in the forest but, of course, no one was there.

"We cannot just drop him here," I told Osande.

"Why not?" she said. "It only makes sense to put him where we picked him up."

"Not really," I disagreed. "He would be alone here out in the middle of nowhere. No way to return to his home. He would starve to death and possibly something would eat him."

She did not much care, which was easy to see. Humans were only slightly higher than other surface primates to Osande. In fact, she viewed them as a cancer upon the planet, though she knew well that we needed them for reproductive materials. I, on the other hand, saw them as budding intelligent beings. All sentient species start out as lower organisms, usually, if allowed the millions of rotations necessary to develop to higher levels. It was not the fault of humans that they had been kick-started by our own ancestors.

"Where then should we leave him?" Osande asked.

We floated around the area and out of the forest. "Somewhere near a town," I said. "Look, there, a fuel station for their vehicles. There is a booth thing there for one of their communication devices. He can call for aid."

Without commenting, she lowered the rover, opened the under door in Bay One and used the beam to lower him to the ground. "I put him on the road," she explained. "Possibly a vehicle will come by and pick him up."

"Or run him over," I commented.

She did not answer.

I took one last look at this weakened human, wished him much good fortune, and we soared back to home base.

It was sometime later when, while monitoring surface media, that it came to our attention that Traviswalton's return was causing a stir. "Listen, will you?" I said to Osande, but she was not interested. And so, I kept watching and listening myself.

It ensued that many different groups were involved, including police, UFO clubs and investigators, the military, and what is referred to as "Hollywood." Apparently, the males he had been with were forced to take various tests to gauge whether they had murdered our detainee. Traviswalton himself told different versions of his experience and Hollywood was making a "movie," supposedly of his story, which was most amusing.

"Osande," I said, forcing my sister to listen. "It seems that the rovers are much larger than they are, and that we have vast containers on them containing human bodies encased in a jelly-like substance. And the clones resemble extremely ugly human embryos!"

"Humans do have imaginations," she said. "I will give them that."

# About the Author

Margaret Karmazin's credits include over 200 stories published in American, Canadian, British, Australian, Indian and European literary and SF magazines, including Rosebud, Chrysalis Reader, North Atlantic Review, Mobius, Confrontation, Pennsylvania Review, The Speculative Edge, Aphelion and Another Realm. Her stories in The MacGuffin, Eureka Literary Magazine, Licking River Review and Mobius were nominated for Pushcart awards. She has stories included in several anthologies, and has published a YA novel, *Replacing Fiona*, a children's book, *Flick-Flick & Dreamer,* and a collection of short stories, *Risk.*

# Incident on Marchen Road

by
Eldon Litchfield

# Incident on Marchen Road

**W**hat the hell caused this mess?"

Officer Joe Moody sighed. Every new arrival asked the same question. The flashing lights of the ambulance and the squad cars danced on the nighttime tree line bordering the road, creating a strobing clash of shadows. He could feel a headache coming on.

"This doesn't make any sense," he said to himself.

"Joe, get over here. It gets weirder."

Moody made his way to his partner, Jack Nimble, trying not to slip in the yellow pulp while side-stepping enormous chunks of pumpkin. Giant seeds were everywhere. It smelled like a prank-smashing of a Halloween jack-o-lantern times a thousand.

"Look at this," Nimble said. "Dead mice right in the middle of this mush. What do you make of all this?"

Moody shook his head. "I can't."

"How's the driver doin'?"

Moody glanced over to the ambulance crew tending to the man. Officer Jane Quick was there asking questions. She nodded to the man then walked toward them.

He waited for her report.

"A bump on the head, scratches from the shattered windshield, a sprained wrist, and a bit shook up. He's lucky." All three officers looked at the driver's totaled pickup. The once-black truck was now mostly yellow and orange. Chunks of pumpkin shell were embedded in the grill and windshield. One wheel was missing.

"He says he was driving home from a late movie around midnight. A stretch limo was in the opposite lane swerving, there was a flash of multicolored light, and then there was a giant pumpkin rolling toward him."

Moody gestured around. "Yeah, plenty of evidence of that."

"He freaked out and couldn't stop, hit it head-on. I'm judging he was doing 40, maybe 50 miles an hour. I didn't detect an alcohol smell. Paramedics don't think he's on anything, but you never know."

Nimble gasped. "Good God, there's a hand sticking out of the pumpkin!"

Moody looked to where Nimble was pointing. An arm covered in yellow pulp and seeds was sticking out of a gap in a piece of shell. They ran over, and two paramedics quickly joined them, all cursing as they slid and shuffled in the wet debris.

Moody and the officers removed the thick pumpkin to reveal the mangled body of a woman. Nimble turned around, collapsing to the ground as his stomach cast out his last meal. The EMTs descended on the body.

"Jesus, she's a wreck. It doesn't look good."

"Is that glass embedded in her right foot?"

"She's got what looks like dirt or soot around her face."

"Huh, she's dressed like a supplicant."

"A what?"

"Y'know, an insolvent, a down-and-out, a poor person. You can tell by the calluses on her hands that she works hard for a living."

Moody and Quick backed away, allowing the paramedics to work.

Moody scanned the night sky.

"What are you looking for?" asked Quick.

Moody snorted. "UFOs? Other vegetables? Any clue. It just doesn't make sense."

"Look over there." Quick gestured to the sideroad.

Moody saw an elderly woman clutching a velvet blue bag. A warped stick crowned with a metallic five-pointed star stuck out of the top. She looked like she had come from a costume party, with a pointed hat supporting bright feathers and wearing a dress fit for performing ballet. She was wringing her pale hands while mumbling. He caught some of what she said as he approached her.

"I did say *before* midnight, didn't I? Not *at* midnight. Leave *before* twelve, I said. I'm certain. I did, didn't I? I did say the right thing, didn't I?"

Moody started to ask her a question, but then noticed someone slowly approaching.

A man in a tux, a mix of Timothée Chalamet and Cary Grant with a sprinkling of Clooney, stared at the paramedics' efforts with the injured woman. In his hands was what appeared to be a ladies' shoe.

He spoke. "Why did she run? Why?"

Moody motioned to Quick and gestured to the old woman before heading to the man with the shoe.

"Sir, what's your name?"

The man's glazed eyes regained focus. "Oh. Yeah, I'll answer your questions. But I want to call my attorney first." He dropped the shoe and walked away while digging for a cell phone in his suit pocket.

Moody recognized the man from the news. Some celebrity who was hosting a grand event downtown this evening, a benefit for the underprivileged. "Say, aren't you that—?"

The man turned around. "Yeah, just… I'll help, any way I can, but let's not talk to the press right yet. Please? No TMZ."

Moody shrugged. "I can't promise anything. There's a giant pumpkin involved."

Moody picked up the dropped shoe. It was a lady's dress pump, made of glass, designed for the left foot.

Officer Quick ran up. "That old woman disappeared. Don't know how she could have moved so fast but—"

"Put out an APB on her," he said. "She might have some answers."

"Okay, a look out for an elderly woman wearing a leotard and a tutu and a lot of feathers. Shouldn't be too hard to miss."

Moody sighed. "Don't believe we'll will find her but send it out just in case. I don't think we'll solve this one. This is one for the books."

# About the Author

Eldon Litchfield writes from Winston-Salem, North Carolina. He spends his time researching bits of old lore and legends and on weekends busies himself writing deep into the night. He writes a little science-fiction, a bit of fantasy, some humor, and a lot of horror. You can visit him at eldonlitchfield.com (warning, the site is very much a work in progress. It's like going through an abandoned attic. Things are scattered everywhere.). By the way, he doesn't like writing Bio's, because he's never sure what to say.

# Bale 13
## by
## Chad Barger

# Bale 13

The Texas sun was high and beaming, the afternoon green and heavy. Hotter than usual for the first weekend of summer.

"Coleman's dad said there's a creeper on the loose and that's why they can't find Lindy Martinez," Scotty said and passed his Zebco fishing pole through the middle two strands of barbed wire.

Thomas took it. Scotty climbed over and joined him on the other side. They marched through the freshly shredded hay meadow toward Bison Creek.

"Well, Coleman's dad's a good guy, and I trust him alright since they go to our church, but the reason they can't find Lindy Martinez is because her dad's a drunk and he lets her uncles touch her for twenty dollars," Thomas said, and they both looked over at the Martinez trailer house.

It stood baby blue and silent, shrouded under a canopy of ancient oaks. Two red hens pecked at the bare brown ground around an iron barbeque pit. A glint of sunlight rippled back to them from the foil-lined kitchen window.

"She ran away. That's what happened," Thomas said.

"Come on, let's go," Scotty said and tugged at Thomas's shirt sleeve.

Once they were out of sight of the trailer house, Scotty looked down at his feet and said, "You don't know that."

"I do know that. I'm fourteen. I know stuff. Jaxon Potter told me on the bus. His dad works with Lindy's dad, and he told me he's a no-good drunk and *he's* the creeper."

"Then where did she go?" Scotty said.

"Town probably. Mexicans around here always have cousins and aunts who live in town. She probably called one of them to come get her and snuck out one night. Why do you care so much?" Thomas said.

"I don't know. Guess that's what folks are talking about most, is all," Scotty said and skipped a step to kick the top off a fire ant mound. The uncapped mound swarmed to life. Thousands of angry brown critters scurried in search of an intruder. Scotty swiped his shoe clean.

"Coleman's dad thinks whoever took the Bryans' lab killed her for practice and then got Lindy Martinez too. Said he probly practiced on stray cats first, and then worked himself up to killing a dog, and now he's turning into a snerial killer," Scotty said.

Thomas snorted.

"It's serial killer, doofus, not snerial killer. And a kid your age shouldn't even have that word in his vocabulary. You keep talking like that and I'm gonna tell mom to not let you stay over at Coleman's anymore. There ain't no creeper on the loose, not way out here in the sticks anyway, and you're safe with me, so don't worry. Lindy Martinez ran away to town, and the Bryans' lab got off her chain and got hit on Highway 30. Probably started chasing something and that's how she got all the way to the highway. Then whoever hit her hauled her off to not get caught. That's why they can't find her."

Thomas's eyes cocked to the left as he took inventory, double-checking if this story really jibed with him. Then another piece tacked itself onto the puzzle board in his mind. Scotty didn't know about this one, but a high school girl had her show steer disappear from the 4H barn behind the football field parking lot. Simply up and vanished. *Poof,* twelve hundred pounds of prime Brangus beef gone in the night. And the thing about it was, it wasn't a good show steer by any means, so there was no reason for someone to come take it. Someone from another town, for instance, who was afraid of her beating him out in the show ring. Happened just two weekends before school let out, a couple days before the news about Lindy Martinez rifled through their tiny village community and put everyone on edge.

Scotty didn't say anything more as they wound through the field of freshly dropped round bales. The threat of not seeing Coleman all summer was enough to keep his mouth shut. He counted the bales, twelve perfectly wrapped cylinders resting in the afternoon sunlight, dozing like Hereford bulls. He scraped the tip of his fishing pole along a bale's net wrapping and wondered how the baler got it on there so perfectly.

A brown grasshopper flitted up from its resting spot as the boys came near. Scotty followed the arc of its descent with his eyes and sprinted to where it landed. He cupped his hands over the grasshopper. The bug launched itself into the pad of Scotty's palm and Scotty closed his hand.

"Got a juicy one," Scotty said with a grin.

Thomas flipped open the tacklebox and pulled out an empty baby food jar. He unscrewed the lid and Scotty deposited the grasshopper.

The brown grasshopper brought the biggest catch of the day, a two-pound channel cat with a missing left whisker. Scotty pulled it in from a still nook behind a sunken junk oil barrel, and he squealed with delight as he dragged it onto the bank. They released it from the stringer before going home because they didn't have anything else big enough to keep. Scotty also caught two mud cats and Thomas caught one, all less than a pound.

Eventually, Thomas snagged his line on an underwater cypress knee and decided to give up rather than go through the effort of rigging a new line. He lay on his back and peered up dreamily at the clear evening sky through the bough of the cypress tree. He wondered how many active serial killers there were in the world, and if he'd ever crossed paths with one on their day-to-day, maybe in the sporting aisle in Walmart, or pumping gas at the Chevron.

Scotty came to sit next to him and let out a deep sigh. Thomas tousled his hair. It was time to go home.

They took the same trail home, and when they came to the hay meadow Scotty grabbed Thomas by the wrist and said, "Wait a minute."

"What's that, boss?" Thomas said.

"There's thirteen now," Scotty said.

"What?"

"There's thirteen haybales now. On our way through the first time, I counted them all, and there were only twelve," Scotty said.

"So what? You counted wrong, genius."

"No. I swear. I counted twice," Scotty said.

Thomas counted the bales and Scotty counted again. Thirteen.

"Maybe one of them divided and now there's thirteen. Tell me this, then. Which one is the new one?"

Scotty scanned the bales and shook his head. "No tellin'."

"Forget about it. Come on. Bet you can't get up on top of one," Thomas said and encouraged Scotty with a hearty clap on the back.

Scotty sprinted for the nearest bale and tried to climb up but slid down the side.

Thomas chuckled.

"You'll never get up that way. You gotta come at it from the back or front, not the sides," Thomas said and gripped the top ledge of the bale and planted his boot in the center swirl. "See, this way the hay gives a little and you can make a step with the tip of your foot."

Thomas hiked his trailing leg over and climbed on. Scotty struggled to gain purchase with his hands and kept pulling out wads of hay. Finally, he bore his fingers in deep and made a little tunnel up to his wrist. Then he gripped and was able to climb a couple steps, reach for the netting, and pull himself up.

"Can you see our house from here?" Scotty said.

Thomas craned his neck.

"Not really. Trees in the way. I think that's the top of the tall pine in our front yard, though," Thomas said and pointed.

Scotty surveyed the field and spotted two bales close together, "Think I can jump from that one to that one?"

"No. Bet I can though," Thomas said, lowered himself, and slid down the side.

Scotty raised his arms and jumped. The ground was further than he judged, and his knees crunched up to his chest when he landed. He paused to catch his breath then ran to join Thomas at the double bales.

Thomas gave Scotty a leg-up this time, then said, "Wait for me. We'll go together."

Thomas climbed up and walked to the end where the other bale sat cattycorner about five feet away. He figured he just might make it if he did a perfect superman and gripped the edge of the net wrapping to pull himself the rest of the way. He gave Scotty no chance.

They lined up in sprinter's stances at the edge of the bale and looked at each other.

"Ready?"

"One… Two… Three… GO!"

Thomas dug in deep for three choppy steps, planted his lead leg at the corner, stretched out his arms, and leaped. He made more than he thought, and his chest planted squarely on the crest of the second bale. He grinned and bicycled his legs up and heaved himself over to the top. Triumph. He looked back to find Scotty picking himself up from the ground between the bales and hid his grin.

Scotty stood and wiped the dirt from his knees. "You got in my way, and I slipped."

"I know bud. Sorry about that. Here," Thomas said and crouched to his chest and offered Scotty his arms.

Scotty gripped Thomas's wrists and planted his foot into the bale. An electric current traveled through Thomas's arms and into Scotty's hands. Scotty's eyes widened and he let go. They looked at each other.

"Woah. You feel that?" Thomas said.

"Yeah. It's incredible. What are you doing?"

"Nothing. I swear. It's like it's coming from the haybale. I can feel it coming up through my chest and into your arms when you grab me," Thomas said.

"Do it again," Scotty said and raised his arms.

Thomas reached down and gripped Scotty's wrists and pulled— *zrrrrrrrrrr*. Same. The dull electric current passed through them.

"HA! Kinda tickles," Scotty said.

Thomas pulled with all his strength and the current raised from dull to throbbing. Scotty gained his feet and stood on the bale with Thomas.

"It's weird. I didn't feel anything when I first jumped on," Thomas said, and his eyebrows lowered.

He jogged through his memory and thought maybe he did. Maybe he did get a little jolt but just didn't notice because the wind was knocked out of him when he landed on the bale.

"I bet this is the thirteenth bale. The one that divided," Scotty said.

"Sure is creepy," Thomas said.

Thomas stamped his foot.

*Zap.* This time Scotty saw it. He saw tiny green lightning bolts gather at Thomas's shoe, reach around like fingers, and grip his ankle.

"Ahh, *shit!*"Thomas clutched his ankle and hopped on one leg. Scotty giggled. It reminded him of the cartoons.

"Dude, this is some messed-up stuff. I've never heard of anything like an electrified haybale," Thomas said.

"There's electric eels, right?" Scotty said.

"Yeah, but that's different. That's an animal. They make their own current somehow, inside their bodies with some kind of special parts. This is just a haybale, a big lump of chopped-up grass and weeds," Thomas said and picked at the net wrapping with his fingers. Nothing happened.

"Maybe lightning struck it. Or maybe there's a powerline underneath it," Scotty said.

Thomas cocked his eyebrows and tilted his head. They looked to the sky just above the road across the field, found the row of power lines, and traced it both directions with their eyes. They disappeared off toward Highway 30 to the right, and off toward their forty acres and the Old Trant place to the left, lost behind a tree-skirted fence line in both directions.

"Come on, let's try to push it," Thomas said and slid down the bale.

Scotty slid down also this time.

They both made themselves stiff as iron stakes, dug into the earth with their feet and pushed with outstretched arms and heads lowered. The haybale budged and settled back into place. Thomas counted.

"One… Two… Three—*Push!*"

Scotty grunted. The haybale rocked, swung back— *"Push!"*— rocked, swung back, *"Push!"* rocked, swung back, *"Push!"* rocked, swung back.

It was no use. The most they got it to go was about seven inches. They'd never be able to rock it over without another person, or a tractor. Thomas breathed quick and deep with his hands on his hips. Scotty inspected his fingers for splinters.

"Did you notice?" Scotty said.

"What? That we're about as strong as a couple of Bambi deer?" Thomas said and smiled.

"It didn't shock us when we pushed it," Scotty said. "It didn't get me. Did it shock you?"

"I guess you're right. It didn't. I was kind of waiting for it at first, but it never did," Thomas said.

"I'm getting hungry," Scotty said.

"Yeah. Let's go home. We'll go get the tractor when mom and dad go to work in the morning and bring it out here. We'll flip it for sure with that. I'll even let you drive a bit if you go get the tackle box and poles," Thomas said and nodded toward the gear they left at the first haybale.

Scotty sprinted away for them.

Mom had sausage and mac 'n' cheese ready for them when they got home. Scotty ate at the dinner table and watched SpongeBob. Thomas made his plate, grabbed a slice of bread, and took it outside to eat on the porch. An electric storm gathered on the horizon. Heavy gray clouds billowed and morphed into and out of each other and flashes of white jolted the sky. Some rumbled.

The electric storm turned to rain that night. Scotty came to Thomas's room. A thunderclap woke Thomas, and he saw him there standing in the doorway. Thomas rolled over.

"What is it, bud? Scared from the storm?"

"No." Scotty said. "Can you come look though?"

Thomas kicked away his covers.

They marched across the hall. Scotty dove onto his bed and pinched his fingers to separate two blinds at the window. The curtains were already tucked away and stuffed into the bedrail to keep them open.

"Here. Let me help you," Thomas said and drew the drawstrings to lift the blinds.

They peered through the window. Thomas's eyes widened. There, in the distance, where they were that afternoon, a cylinder of green light climbed up and into the sky. Hazy among the foggy mess of rainclouds, but perfect, round, and crisp when the wind settled.

"Isn't that where bale thirteen is?" Scotty said and moved his finger.

Thomas traced the path with his eyes.

"That's Bison Creek, and over there is the Marinez place, and across from it over there is the power lines, so that weird light has to be coming from the middle, where the haybales are," Scotty said and looked up at Thomas.

Thomas knelt on the bed, wiped their breath from the windowpane, and squinted. Scotty's mapping was spot-on in his estimation. The beam shimmered like plasma. Thomas thought of thousands of tiny jellyfish swimming around in a circle.

"I'mma go get dad," Scotty said and moved to hop off of the bed.

Thomas stopped him with a wave of his hand.

"No. I'll. Just becau…" Thomas stammered, then thought for a moment "I'll just sleep in here with you tonight."

Scotty grabbed his pillows and pulled them to the foot of the bed. They kept the window blinds open and laid there next to each other and watched the green beam of light pulsing in the distance. At every thirty seconds it became bright, bright enough to squint their eyes a smidge, and at the end of the next thirty seconds it was dim again. Thomas saw the storm clouds rolling through the top of the beam and it became longer and shorter with them.

When they woke the next morning, the beam was gone. It was ten thirty. Mom was gone. Dad was gone. Thomas pulled the drawstrings and let the blinds fall to the windowsill. Scotty woke up and lifted one to look out.

"It's gone," Thomas said.

"Are we still going to get the tractor?" Scotty said.

"Yeah. Get dressed," Thomas said.

The mid-morning sky was overcast, the ground mushy. Their backyard was littered with twigs and leaves from the storm. Scotty blasted through the French doors and trotted after Thomas, still pulling his arm through the sleeve of his Spiderman t-shirt.

Thomas patted the back of Scotty's head when he caught up.

"What do you think it is?" Scotty said.

"I don't know. I thought about it all last night and couldn't come up with anything," Thomas said and swiped the tip of his nose with his wrist.

"I bet it's an alien. I bet an alien ship came down and planted that haybale in disguise. I saw something like that on a movie we watched at Coleman's. Or maybe the haybale *is* the ship. It just cloaked itself all over to look like a haybale," Scotty said.

"Yeah. Or maybe the mother ship is up there in the sky where we can't see. Past the clouds. That light beam is how the little ship talks to the big one. And maybe that's what happened to Lindy Martinez too. Whatever's going on in the pasture, I mean. That's what happened to Lindy and the Bryans' lab," Thomas said.

Scotty looked up at Thomas to see if he was just kidding. Thomas looked down to him and didn't smile.

They rounded the corner of the driveway and looked up and studied the sky. They saw nothing but rippling mammatus clouds, after-storm clouds. It looked to Scotty like God layered the heavens with a sheet of billowy bubble wrap.

They came to the barn and heard the rumble of a tractor in the distance. Thomas unlatched the barn door and swung it open. They saw the tractor was missing.

"Aww nuts," Scotty said.

"Yeah. I bet Mr. Trant's using it. I bet a tree fell in the storm and they're using the tractor to pull it off the road and clean up. That happened last time, too," Thomas said. "Don't worry. We're still going to go out there and check it out."

"But we can't flip the haybale without the tractor," Scotty said.

"Yeah. I got another idea," Thomas said.

They marched back to the house, and when they came to the end of the driveway, Thomas pointed to the ground and said, "Wait right here a minute."

Scotty watched Thomas disappear into the house and waited for what he thought was a long time. After a few moments, he realized he didn't have to stand in that exact spot the whole while, so he jogged over to the chicken coop, picked up his football, and punted it across the yard. Then he chased the ball down and spun it up into the air.

When Thomas re-appeared through the French doors, Scotty's jaw went slack. Thomas was carrying Dad's hunting rifle, The Stinger, over his shoulder, soldier style. The Stinger was Dad's treasured Winchester Model 70, a bolt action .243 they'd seen Dad drop a coyote with, from at least three football fields away in the back pasture.

"Ohhhhh. Dad said—" Scotty began.

"I don't care what Dad said." Thomas cut him off short. "There's something spooky going on around here, and we're not gonna get caught with our pants down."

The unexpected turn of phrase brought a smirk to Scotty's face. Then the smirk turned into another look and Thomas didn't have to ask to know what was on Scotty's mind.

"Yes. I'll let you shoot it. Once. If we have time," he said.

Scotty spiked the football and did a little knee-wiggling celebration dance.

They crossed the lawn and entered the woods that separated their place from the hay meadow, through a clearing in a group of holly bushes. The woods looked different after the rainstorm, fuller. The wind snapped dead branches up high, and they leaned to rest on lower ones. A dead hackberry engulfed the span of the trail lengthwise in one place. Smaller bunches of leaves were strewn across the trail in others.

Thomas kept lookout for rabbits and deer as they traveled. Something about carrying a rifle heightened his senses, made his eyes keen. He saw none. Only one squirrel, and several birds chattering back and forth— *"Hey, did you see my house? It got smashed to bits..." "Yeah, you seen mine?"*

The clearing twined into view, and they came to the barbed wire fence. Thomas stripped the leather strap from his shoulder and instructed Scotty to pass the rifle to him, *carefully*, when he got to the other side. Scotty held it like a baby. Thomas climbed over and reached his hands through the middle two strands of barbed wire. Scotty placed the rifle in them and strung the strap across on top. Scotty climbed over and joined him on the other side.

They marched through the freshly-mown hay meadow toward Bison Creek. There was no beam of light. Scotty counted the haybales and came to the same figure, thirteen. Thomas looked up at the sky. There was no alien spaceship hovering up there. Only clouds. Bubbly clouds.

They circled bale thirteen at a wide distance and came to where they stood twenty feet away, looking directly at the middle swirl. Thomas reached into his pocket and the brass cartridges jangled. He lowered the tip of the barrel, pulled back the bolt, and slid it home, *click-clack*.

"Do you think Dad counts his bullets?" Scotty said.

Thomas didn't answer. He raised the rifle, lined the sights up with the swirl of the haybale, drew a breath, and squeezed the trigger.

*KER-CHAK! TINK! chak chak chak chak.*

Thomas saw a flicker of green forcefield surround the bale, a shattering of something electric.

A group of grackles took flight from the Bison Creek side of the meadow.

Thomas heard a thud. He looked back and saw Scotty lying on his back, arms spread, a slick red dot growing just above his left eyebrow.

Thomas dropped the rifle.

# About the Author

Chad Barger lives on a small hobby farm in the middle of Texas with his lovely wife, two kids, and two dogs. He enjoys playing video games, reading, and outdoor adventures.

# The *Polybius* Truth

### by
### DW Milton

# The *Polybius* Truth

**C**lark opened the back door. The refrigerator-sized box barely fit on the dolly, taking Clark and the deliveryman 10 minutes to wedge it through the doorframe. Once it was inside, Clark tipped the man five dollars while hustling him out the door.

Alone, he could barely control his excitement, wanting to rip into the wrapping like a kid on Christmas morning. Clark checked his watch again.

*Where was John?*

John was as much a fan as Clark, but not a believer.

The box sat in the middle of the room surrounded by other arcade video games. Clark and John were aficionados, having spent years playing the games, and now they refurbished them. The new arrival inside the unassuming cardboard was a video gamer's Holy Grail, and it represented a quest that had begun 15 years ago.

Clark glanced at the wall where, framed, was an alleged letter from the FBI dated November 3, 2017. He knew the correspondence by heart.

*This is in response to your freedom of information act (FOI) request regarding the video game Polybius.*

The letter described the FBI search of the central records system resulting in no filed records regarding the video game *Polybius.*

The letter concluded: *This is a standard notification that is given to all requesters and should not be taken as an indication that excluded records do, or do not, exist.*

Clark found that last part interesting considering that the game, whose existence the FBI could or could not verify, stood before him.

A commotion outside; the back door opened with a rush of wind, noise, and limbs.

John was tall, lanky, and always tripping over his ridiculous feet. "Is it here? Why didn't you call me?" Stopping short, he almost tumbled headfirst into the box.

Clark dodged, "Because you never answer your mobile. You were supposed to be here an hour ago."

"I know. But I am here now; what are you waiting for!"

Clark handed him the box cutter. "You found it. You do the honors."

John's lopsided grin spread.

Since they had been kids haunting their local arcade, this game had such a convoluted history that it was hard not to buy into the hype. Both had heard the stories. Next to the framed letter was a photocopied article from a popular gamer's mag that also declared the existence of the game to be inconclusive.

After the article hit the stands, several people claimed that they were involved in the development of the game. Internet chat rooms were on fire—some folks claiming foul while others wanted to know more.

The big break happened when John tracked down one of the supposed programmers.

Initially, John the skeptic, also called their bluff claiming that, back in the 1980s, the cutting-edge graphics and intense gameplay that reportedly caused the detrimental side effects including, but not limited to, hallucinations and seizures, were impossible. No matter how cool, there was no such thing as a *TRON*. Gaming tech and code simply could not affect player neurological functioning, nor beam anyone inside a game.

An internet chat room war ensued. Vulgarities and insults flew. John threw down a gauntlet. "You can claim all that you want, but until I see it, I won't believe it."

Three days later, a posted letter arrived at the store. Inside was a faded Polaroid of the game console that now sat in the store's back room.

The Polaroid, also framed, hung on the other side of the letter completing their Holy Trinity.

Clark took the packaging outside to the dumpster while John grabbed his toolbox. Before beginning, both revered the cabinet, pilgrims paying homage to a long-lost shrine.

"Shall we?" Clark leaned over the small filing cabinet to plug in the game.

"Wait! Use the surge protector. Remember how that last one fried the breakers."

Clark obliged and unplugged an idle printer. The three-pronged plug trembled in his hand. He inserted it. John, who was crouched at the back of the game cabinet, flipped the small black switch. Both jumped forward in order to view the screen.

Nothing—not a blip, a flash or a puff of life.

"Well," sighed Clark, "at least it didn't catch fire."

"Who was Polybius again?" John teased. "Patron saint of horse hockey?"

"Greek philosopher," Clark groaned. "He taught that we can learn from our history."

"You mean like, from our mistakes? Like buying this piece of crap." John inserted his Phillips-head, exerting the slightest pressure and increasing until the screw rotated left.

Forty-five minutes later, the unnaturally-black panels leaned against the back wall of the shop. John had his head in the spine of the console, looking up. Wires and boards tickled and scratched his ears. Sweat beaded his brow.

Clark removed the glass covering the monitor to check connections.

"What's this?" Clark fingered a newer, pliable cable very different from the older worn ones. The cable looked like a fiber optic cable. He pulled on it. John winced as a small back device slipped down and clipped his forehead.

He grabbed his assailant, "What's this?"

"You okay? I didn't think…" Clark stopped. "Is that a spy camera?"

The tiny cylinder had a lens-like eye and a short tail linking it to the molded cabinet. Clark had dislodged it from a matching groove tucked in the upper corner where it perched, providing a bird's eye view of the gamer.

John traced the fiber optics into the console's belly where nestled behind circuit boards was a small device that looked like a USB stick.

"I'll bet my vintage *Arcade1Up Super PAC-MAN Countercade* this is the recording device."

"Yeah, but what do you think it records?"

Clark recalled a rumor he never believed—men in black suits, sunglasses, and tiny earpieces, who made midnight visits to closed arcades. In his mind, what would Will Smith and Tommy Lee be doing in arcades…unless? Clark looked at the devices more carefully. Both were connected via what looked like fiber optic cables, yet…

John fiddled with the cables trying, unsuccessfully, to remove the system.

"How can this be?" John followed the snaking cables into the machine where they disappeared into the streamline molding of the cabinet. "It's part of the cabinet, but…"

After years of friendship, Clark finished his sentence. "This technology did not exist in the 1980s. Hell, it's unusual for the 2020s."

John moved to the front of the game. Like the flash drive, the camera cable was embedded. "This had to be placed during the manufacturing, which is not possible."

Clark grabbed a scalpel blade and peeled back the cable skin. Inside, the contents of the cable were unlike anything either of them had seen before.

A moment then, "Holy cow, I know what this is!" Clark hustled over to the desktop computer and opened it to the web. "I saw one of these at that tech conference we went to last fall."

Fingers flying over the keyboard, he pulled up the conference agenda. "Here," pointing at the screen. "It is a new fiber optic that blows broadband out of the water. Everything is transmitted on photons, but they somehow manipulate the photons, twisting them so that they not only carry more 1s and 0s but also carry the information faster, without wires and without interference."

"Okay, cool," John commented, "but again, this thing was built the 1980s. You are telling me about tech that is still in its infancy now, more than 40 years later."

Clark lost his cool. "I told you! This has got to be some sort of government-sanctioned alien experiment!"

John had heard all Clark's conspiracy theories before. Circling back around the console cabinet, he touched the recording device. Gingerly, he slid the small rectangular box off the black cord. It looked like any flash drive from any office supply store. He shoved Clark over to get to the tower and inserted the drive. "Here goes nothing."

At first, the mainframe did not detect the device. Following a number of error notices and a few choice four-letter words, John finally forced the recognition.

"You kiss your mother with that mouth?" Clark grinned.

John ignored him.

The flash drive contained thirteen video files time-stamped during the month of April in the year 1982.

The only time either John or Clark left the computer was for bathroom breaks and a quick run to the front door for their pizza delivery. Clark gave their usual delivery guy, Seth, an unusually large tip, leaving Seth suspicious as Clark was a well-known tightwad.

What kept them glued to the screen were the multitude of teenagers dressed in dayglow, pastel *Izods,* or torn heavy metal swag and faded bandannas playing the game non-stop. Quarter after quarter, hour after hour, the teens stood, leaned, slapped, and kicked the machine while they gamed their afternoons away. Bitten by the nostalgia bug, both men sat through half of the videos lost in a haze of memories.

"Look at her!" John exclaimed when a blonde with a side ponytail, and a mesh black crop top revealing a black lace bra, twirled by the game. "She looks just like Tiffany Benedetto." Tiffany had also emulated Madonna in her *Lucky Star* days. John had raging crushes on both women.

What happened next was exceptional. Players and passersby always appeared well-behaved. Occasionally, there was some smack talk, but nothing major. Yet, in this video, it was obvious the arcade had just opened. Before the *Madonna-wannabe* walked by, the place seemed empty, and the time stamp indicated it was late morning. Schools would still be in session.

In the previous videos, it was not until the afternoon that kids would come and go. Regulars stopped and played, talked with friends, and moved on. This time, there seemed to be a disturbance even before anyone came into view.

"I am going to kick your sorry ass! That's my game and I am going to play it for as long as I want to!" A headbanger with a torn jean jacket and long hair came into view. He reached into his back pocket and took something out of it. On the audio, Clark and John heard a metallic click.

They had watched him play the video game many times,

commenting how much he reminded them of Judd Nelson in *The Breakfast Club*. During the Judd's gameplay his expression intensified. Clark noticed that his expression changed. His emotions seemed to dampen. Worse, the boy had beautiful robin's-egg blue eyes, but the longer he played, Clark saw his pupils dilate so wide that the blue irises turned black. Clark couldn't tell for sure, but there were times when the kid looked like he began to drool leaving puddles of saliva on the glass. It was just like the internet drabble Clark read during his research, describing the alleged detrimental side effects of playing the game: marathon gameplay, paranoia, erratic and sometimes violent behavior at the machine.

Clark looked closer. "Is that a switch blade?"

Another boy, dressed like another John Hughes movie, stepped into view. He was as tall as the other was but beefier.

"Jake Ryan," muttered John. Both men watched, mesmerized. The Judd Nelson kid stood his ground, back to the game, knife out. Jake stepped forward to challenge him.

"Step away," Judd warned. "The *Grey Ones* only want me to play, no one else. Not you or your preppy asses. Get lost!"

The camera caught two other preppies tight in the background.

"James Spader and Eric Stoltz."

John agreed.

Jake squared his shoulders and then shrugged Judd off. The preppies followed, leaving Judd and the game. Judd waited before clicking the knife back into its place before turning back to his game.

"What the hell was that?" John leaned back in his chair, exhausted.

"I am not sure." Clark watched the Judd Nelson kid play, black pupils consuming the brilliant blue. Clark looked at John. "What did he mean by the *Grey Ones*?"

Four more hours of banal video left Clark irritable and John with a headache.

"There's nothing more but a bunch of Quarter Jockeys

wasting away their lunch money."

A new set of teenagers dressed like Bill and Ted swarmed in, hogging the machine.

Clark was about ready to switch the computer off and close up for the night when he heard the not-as-attractive-as-Keanu Ted say, "Do you think Brian really stabbed him?"

Even a snoozing John sat up at the comment.

Bill bent to deposit his change and the now familiar electronic game jingle played.

"Yeah dude, totally! I heard he stabbed him like a hundred times. It was totally gnarly. Like blood everywhere."

"Cool," Ted replied as the game began.

John looked at Clark. "You think the game had anything to do with it?"

Clark got up and touched the black monolith in the center of the room. "What if we could find a newspaper clipping? If there was a stabbing, it had to be reported, right?"

"Yeah sure, but we don't even know where this happened."

"Wait," Clark returned to the monitor, scanning the screen. "There," he pointed. "Behind Ted, what's that?"

"Looks like a flyer for a county fair or something." John paused the video.

"Can you enlarge it?"

"Done." John was already tapping away at the keyboard, shifting the image, enlarging the space behind Ted's left shoulder where pegged into a bulletin board was a yellow paper flyer. After some tweaking and refocusing, it read:

*DuPage County Fair April 23-26, 1982*

"Oh man, there has got to be a hundred DuPage Counties in the US," Clark complained.

John continued typing. "Nope, just one."

Clark did a double take. "Where?"

"Illinois. Just outside of Chicago."

"You are kidding me. Isn't that where the guy who sold us the game lives?"

John grunted. "Chicago, yeah, or at least that's where I sent the money."

Clark's mind was racing. He closed his eyes trying to picture the confrontation between Judd and Jake. "Didn't one of the preppies have a sweatshirt with a school name?"

"Just a moment, yeah." John reversed the video. "There." He stopped the feed. *"Naperville Redhawks."*

Clark was excited. "Naperville? It's about a four-hour drive. I could check it out and…"

A flash on the screen. A set of huge black eyes, then a warm glow of snow particles.

"What was that?" John snatched his hand away from the mouse as if it was radioactive.

John and Clark looked at each other.

John came to the shop early the next day, before Clark headed out. He wanted to get another look at that video. Both promised to call the other if they learned anything new, John begrudgingly. John hated cell phones, believing they caused brain cancer.

Clark was right; the drive took about four hours with traffic, so he arrived around lunch. The newspaper office was closed for the hour, but the library was not.

Inside, Clark charmed the librarian into pointing out the antique microfiche viewer and then impressed her with his knowledge of how to use it.

"So many young people nowadays expect everything to be digital, just swipe your finger, *voila.*" She leaned in as if to confide her darkest secret. "In fact, I refuse to scan things if I don't have to."

Not wanting to lose her good will, Clark smiled.

Two hours later, Clark found an article. Two Naperville high school boys, Brian Kellerman and the high school quarterback Michael Annalee, had gotten into an altercation, as he and John suspected. Kellerman, the Judd Nelson of the local rat pack, pulled a knife and stabbed Annalee 10 times before the cops shot him.

The level of violence was surprising. Local police said that

Kellerman, after stabbing Annalee, charged them. He succeeded in stabbing a patrolman in the shoulder before officers took him down.

The article elaborated that Kellerman had been acting strange, appearing to respond to voices and threatening others. Although there had been no previous discourse between the teenagers as they traveled in different social circles, recently both had frequented the local gaming arcade, *Quarters Unknown*.

Friends of the deceased athlete mentioned that they were surprised that Annalee, who had never shown an interest in video games before, was spending increasing amounts of time at the arcade. On the other hand, Kellerman was a fixture at *Quarters Unknown*. There were also rampant rumors of Kellerman extorting and bullying some of the younger patrons; however, charges were never filed. Arcade owner Jimmy Reitman was unavailable for comment.

Clark scanned additional articles before he found one describing another unusual occurrence in the sleepy town. A local fisherman discovered Jimmy Reitman, the owner of the *Quarters Unknown* arcade, floating in the local creek. Despite no official investigation, the death was ruled an accident and the case closed.

He printed the relevant articles, tucking them into his notebook and said his good-byes to the librarian before hurrying out to the street. He needed to call John.

On the street, Clark paused at the light to take out his phone. Somehow, he had missed a text from John.

It read *I played the game.*

Why didn't John call; that was the deal?

The light had changed but Clark missed it. He dialed John's phone. The next green cycle, he ran the three blocks to his car.

Breathless, "Come on, pick up!"

While John's phone rang, Clark jumped in and switched on the ignition. Still waiting, he cursed John and his fear of a brain tumor then hung up and tried the shop phone.

The call went unanswered, but the phone beeped announcing a new text.

*There is more to the video.*

Clark was furious.

Then, *Find someone who played the game and show them this.*

The phone beeped a third time and an MP4 video file appeared on the screen. With it was the text: *Must obey The Grey Ones.*

Kellerman had mentioned *The Grey Ones* when threatening Annalee. Were they part of this conspiracy? Clark, a believer, had seen their images a million times on alien encounter websites, TV shows and movies, and now John was texting *The Grey Ones.*

Clark was about to key up the MP4 file to view it when the phone beeped.

*DO NOT WATCH THE VIDEO YOURSELF!!!!!!!!!!!!*

He looked at the screen in disbelief. What the hell was John talking about telling him to not watch what was probably the closest he had ever come to being part of a bona fide alien conspiracy. Not just reading about it online. Not just hearing about it on a podcast *but* discovering, investigating and, (hopefully) proving one of the longest running urban legends in the gaming world. Their world.

"Get bent, John!" Clark moved his finger over the file.

The phone beeped.

*PLEASE DO NOT WATCH IT!! I AM BEGGING YOU!!!*

Clark stared at the screen, his finger hovering. "Fine!" he hollered at the device using his finger instead to call John's phone; this time it went directly to voice mail.

Exasperated, Clark threw down the phone, grabbed the steering wheel and screamed. John was a pain in the ass most of the time, but why choose now of all times to be a total royal jerk? Clark gazed at the car roof. A fold in the fabric had a long, lean finger-like look. The crease crawled up the roof blending into an old stain. The stain was ovoid, a face with two large hollow eyes, a rudimentary nose and a slit mouth. A large head tapering into an inhuman chin. The fold rippled and the finger extended down, reaching.

Clark screamed, this time in terror, hands covering his eyes. He was going to have a heart attack and die while sitting here in this unfamiliar parking lot in this strange town while his best friend in the world dodged his calls feeding him some bullarky about *not* watching possibly the most important video in the history of the world!

Realizing the idiocy of his situation, he laughed, yet he was still afraid of opening his eyes.

A sharp knock on his window shocked them open. A

policeman stood next to his door. Flustered, Clark searched for the handle then rolled down the glass to a stern face shaded by mirrored lenses.

"Are you alright, sir?" The voice was deep and concerned.

"I…I think so. I was trying to get in touch with someone, but he won't answer."

"Would you mind turning off the vehicle and stepping out of the car, sir?"

Clark obliged.

"May I see your license and registration, please, sir?"

Clark fumbled with his wallet.

"Stay here please, Mr. Watson."

Clark paced while the officer returned to his patrol car. Outside the cramped car, Clark calmed but his thoughts buzzed of the video game, the newspaper articles and John's texts: *I played; There is more; Find someone; Show them; Must obey the Grey Ones.*

The officer returned, handing Clark his identification. "You sure you are okay? You looked pretty rattled there."

"Yeah, yeah," Clark reassured. "My buddy, he can drive anyone half mad sometimes." Then he decided to try a hunch. "Maybe you can help me. I am looking for the Annalee family. Would they still be in town?

"The Annalees? I haven't heard that name for a while." The officer rubbed his chin. "I knew 'em. Went to high school with Mike."

Clark's eyes lit up. Keeping it causal, gathering his confidence, "You knew Mike? He was one of the boys involved in that stabbing incident some years back."

The officer's face crumpled. "Played football with him. Mike was a good guy. He didn't do nothing to Kellerman. That kid just went plain crazy."

"I'm sorry." Clark genuinely was. "You must have been close."

The officer nodded.

"So, uh, is anyone else still around."

The officer shook his head. "Well, you still mean mentally? After Mike was killed, his kid brother Todd kind of lost it. He kept saying that some video game poisoned their minds and made them fight. It was bad. I mean he was utterly delusional saying that *the Grey People…*" The officer's radio crackled. "Sorry, I got to take this."

Clark's hope sank until before leaving the officer said, "They had him committed."

Clark looked up, "What?"

"Todd's parents. They admitted him to Elgin. Poor kid lost his brother, then lost his mind." The officer disappeared into his vehicle and drove off.

Ducking back into his car, Clark grabbed his cell phone and searched *mental hospital* and *Elgin* with immediate results for Elgin Mental Health Center, located in Elgin, IL. Before pulling out of the parking lot, he had his route and time of arrival.

Visiting hours ended in a half hour, so Clark told a small white lie in order to see Todd, who was still an inpatient.

The nurse explained as they walked the brightly lit corridor, "It will be good for Todd to see some family."

"Well, it's been a while so I am not sure he will remember me," Clark fibbed.

"No worries," the nurse reassured. "When he arrived, he was catatonic; but over the last few years he's grown more responsive, follows commands, and can give simple responses. It's like his brain had to reboot."

In the dayroom, a thin, balding Todd Annalee sat alone at a table looking out the picture window.

The nurse guided Clark over to introduce them. "Todd, this is your cousin Clark. Do you remember Clark? He has come to see you. Say hello, Todd."

From behind fishbowl glasses, an empty set of faded blue eyes peered at Clark's brown ones. Clark's hopes dipped again. This would be a short visit.

Todd Annalee turned back to his window.

The nurse frowned. "I'll leave you to get reacquainted."

Clark stood helpless, wanting to follow the nurse. Instead, he sat next to Todd noticing the view. "It's lovely."

They sat silent. Clark fumbled with his phone in his pocket and chewed on his lower lip. He decided to play it straight.

He turned, facing Todd. "I liked to play videogames when I was a kid. Did you like to play videogames too?"

With no change in his expression, Todd remained mute.

"Did you ever play at the *Quarters Unknown* arcade in town?"

Todd shifted slightly in his chair.

Clark took a deep breath. "Did you ever play *Polybius*?"

Although the sun was out and the sky was clear, a darkness slid in as if a cloud was passing. Todd's left hand compulsively tugged at the armrest, warping the plastic back and forth. Bending it, creating a white crease in the material. Clark could not stop staring; it resembled an extended finger.

The conspiracy theorist in Clark took it as a sign; he keyed up the video. Although he was unsure what he was asking, he asked anyway. Unable to keep the desperation out of his voice, he said, "Todd, can you help me, I mean, John? I need you to watch this. He…my friend…sent it, and I think he's in trouble because of it."

Clark put the phone in Todd's hands. Leaning over, Clark tapped the arrow then enlarged the image to full. The screen remained dark for a moment before a light like a camera flash but infinitely brighter illuminated Todd's face. Todd's blue eyes revivified—a long-extinguished flame ignited.

Clark tried to heed John's warning, but he was mesmerized. At first, the light was comforting and familiar. Clark could feel its warmth. As it grew, so did a small bubble in the center of the display. The picture focused on the iridescent bubble blossoming forth as if from a child's lips. The bubble expanded. Bigger, Bigger. Immense.

The view transformed to within the bubble. It encompassed them; nourished and protected them from the surrounding darkness. Through the transparent surface, Clark saw streaks of light race by at unfathomable speeds, swirls of glowing galaxies rotating endlessly before being swallowed by supermassive black holes. Blasts of cosmic energy exploding from quasars threatened to blind him as they passed. Inside the bubble, he felt an unbearable lightness soon replaced by the tug of immeasurable gravity.

The image on the screen dimmed to black—profound and limitless. The blackness consumed them. An oily ink that stared back. Clark's hand trembled holding the phone. He wanted to drop it and run screaming from the room; instead, he remained frozen to his chair.

He could hear Todd shudder, but Clark's gaze was fixed. The blackness retreated, shifted. A second orb appeared. Two huge black eyes set in a ridiculously large head covered by a sickly grey skin. A long thin alien finger pointed at them through the display.

Todd, who had been hyperventilating with the reveal of the second eye, began screaming.

Paralysis broken, Clark swiped the image off the screen and tucked the phone back in his pocket. Before he could even attempt to calm Todd, the nurse and a large orderly entered the dayroom.

The nurse curtly asked Clark to leave.

In the parking lot of the hospital, a discombobulated Clark did not see the two unmarked cars parked at the back of the lot. Clark did not observe the two occupants of the first car enter the hospital. He also did not notice the second car follow him out onto the highway.

Still reeling, Clark pulled into a fast-food drive-thru. Maybe some food would calm his nerves. John was still not answering his phone and Clark's imagination shifted into high gear. While munching on his hamburger, Clark opened up his phone to the video. Four minutes remained.

Clark was not certain he wanted to disobey John, but his curiosity and the obvious eyes of the grey thing…alien…whatever was on the screen, had definitely hit home with Todd. Clark could still hear Todd's hysteria reverberating in his ears. Hamburger done with only a few cold fries left, Clark hit the arrow and the video resumed.

The inhumanly long finger had an extra joint but no nail. The view panned out and four of the grey entities stood next to the *Polybius* video arcade game. Clark did a quick measurement; if the game cabinet was the same one in his shop, these creatures were barely 4 feet tall. A flash of Spielberg's *Close Encounters* passed through his mind; maybe the auteur was closer to truth than fiction.

Never once did Clark *not* believe what he was seeing could be real. He was not a videophile like John and had no idea how someone could fake this. Then whatever it was, it got weird. The warm light returned but with a bite. It pulsed. Slowly. Rhythmically. Hypnotically. Painfully, penetrating and permeating into his brain.

The faces of *The Grey Ones* blurred. Clark's lids felt heavy. His brain fogged. His head nodded.

Clark awoke in his car, in the parking lot of the restaurant, in the dark. His neck was stiff, left foot numb. He rubbed his eyes then checked his phone. Almost two hours lost, and he'd missed two calls from John. Confused, he swiped the screen, calling John back.

John answered, his voice cold and flat. "I told you not to watch the video."

"What? Where have you been? I have been trying to reach you for hours."

"Why, Clark? Why did you watch it?"

Clark huffed, "How do you even know that I did?"

"They told me!" John shouted. "Now I must obey."

"Who, John, obey who?"

John hung up before answering.

Furious, Clark started the car. He and John were going to have words when he got to the shop. Clark was sick of this crap.

The unmarked car pulled out of the parking lot after Clark but turned onto the highway, heading in the opposite direction.

It was well after midnight when Clark arrived. The back alley was empty except for John's car.

Clark unlocked and opened the door, "John! Hey, John! Are you here?"

The lights were off when Clark entered but the video game *Polybius*, still in the center of the room, emanated a warm glow. Clark halted. *Déjà vu.* The light, the warmth; now there was a hum.

The monitor screen was alive, advertising *game on.* Distracted, Clark moved to the console. The entire cabinet radiated not only the light but also the sound. The marquee, the molding, each side art, and the monitor pulsed. He touched the control panel, fingers brushing the joystick, triggering endorphins to burst within his brain. The sensation was orgasmic.

"No!" A familiar voice screamed from the corner of the room. "They only want me to play, no one else. Not you!"

Before Clark could turn, his best friend since kindergarten stabbed the Phillips-head screwdriver down, piercing Clark's lung and nicking his aorta, causing fatal internal bleeding. Although the first blow technically killed Clark, John brought the pointed tip down nine more times before stopping.

The men in black suits arrived at the shop and took John into custody. Like many before him, the last twelve hours of continuous play had left John in a near-vegetative state, making him easy to subdue. The lack of investigation, clean up, and cover up of Clark's murder went by the book. Although the protocol was 40 years old and had undergone revision to include confiscation of items not in existence in the 1980s, like cell phones and personal computers, it still served its purpose.

Outside the shop, a man arrived in an inconspicuous white truck to pack up and remove the game, making it ready for delivery to its next owner.

# About the Author

DW Milton is a pen name. The author has a day job but would rather spend her time writing speculative fiction. A transplant from the East Coast to the desert of the Southwest, the author misses the beach, but ten years later still finds the views of the mountains and sunsets inspiring. An avid artist, hiker and cyclist, the author loves movies, videogames and reading any and all kinds of speculative fiction from Cyberpunk and Splatterpunk to Horror and, of course, Science Fiction.

# One Night in New Mexico
by
Christopher Blinn

# One Night in New Mexico

**B**elow is a transcript of my notes, observations and recordings in regards to the series of events that began on Wednesday, July 2, 1947 in Roswell, New Mexico.

You will never know me or who I was. Although you may speculate, your conclusions would be of no importance. The Government has either silenced me permanently or they have me locked away so deep in an Army hospital that, even if you correctly guessed my identity, you would never find me. Besides, if you did, chances are I don't even know who I am anymore.

In retrospect, creating this document of my recollections of that evening was reckless. Not for me, you understand, as I have long since had the need to worry about such matters, but for you the discoverer, the reader, this knowledge could be dangerous. I would suggest you go no further and destroy the papers you're holding. Should you not, it will be obvious why my story, the information below, can never be made public.

My official reports were confiscated, their fate unknown, to me at least. This unofficial account is all that remains of the actual events.

Use your best discretion.

## 0237: Roswell Army Airfield

I received a phone call from Colonel Conroy to respond to unusual activity and civilian reports of an unidentified aircraft. A likely crash scenario.

Now before you think you can solve the mystery of my identity simply by checking Army records to see who was in command of the Roswell base, think again. I was in command of a special detachment whose existence you will not find in any records. We were stationed on the base along with the "regulars" but there was no fraternization. We had training, skills, and orders.

Please don't bother the Major of the 509th Bomb Group if he is still alive. He was never told and never knew the truth.

We had standard procedures for responding to any number of situations. All our calls to this point except one had been drills. The only "live call," as we referred to them, had been a crash as well. The ditched vehicle turned out to be a civilian aircraft, no survivors. Despite our professionalism, this was on all our minds as we deployed with "crash protocol." Another drill.

0251: In less than fifteen minutes we were en route. Coordinates mapped. ETA to site: 0317. Twenty-six minutes. I rode in the lead vehicle, a standard Army jeep, directing the driver. My second in command was behind me in a troop carrier with six men and a driver. A flatbed trailer, hauling lighting that could turn midnight into high noon and a generator that could keep it that way for days, followed third with two more men. An ambulance with two medics took last. Twelve men total. All specialists in one area or another. The troop carrier held our equipment, the latest devices for every contingency the brass could imagine, from measuring radiation levels to photographic gear.

0312: We could see the glow of the crash site as we approached on the only passable route available. Fire intensity was low, indicating any fuel the craft was carrying had not combusted. Smoke was minimal as well. Good conditions for my men as it made the wreckage easier to approach. Lack of a large explosion meant fewer witnesses and less attention. It also lent to the possibility of survivors. The danger was that any unconsumed fuel could ignite at any moment and roast us where we stood. This was our job.

0313: I updated my second in command and instructed the men to stand ready. It looked like we had a "live call."

0317: On scene. The men deployed with practiced efficiency. Two with Geiger counters, each flanked by a man, weapon ready. Two more men joined them with lights that required two hands to hold, a battery pack hung from their backs strung crossways on their chests. The trios separated left and right following the beams from the powerful lights. They stopped thirty feet apart. A scar in the earth marked the distance between the two teams. They waited for orders.

0319: My second and I followed the men. I went right, he took left. I directed them to proceed. The two medics joined us and separated in the same fashion. The two men from the flatbed stood guard with the vehicles.

At this point I will leave out the chronology. Any times I list after we began our search could be inaccurate and only lead to more confusion. The magnitude of the situation quickly became obvious to myself and my men. To their credit they stayed sharp, focused on the mission. Training? No amount of training could prepare a man for what we found.

With lighting equipment not yet established we had only the powerful handhelds to guide us. The trench continued to spread before us, widening as we went. Earth was pushed to the sides, forming a gully I estimated to be about four feet deep. (Although later measurements would put it at closer to six). Burn marks marked the tops of the channel. Scorched by a short but intense heat. There was no sign a fire had burned for any duration causing the discoloration of the sand and soil. Whatever had caused the furrow had been moving and moving fast.

At fifty yards we found the first piece of wreckage. It was too small to make a guess at what type of metal it was or what type of craft it may have originated from.

We moved slowly, never advancing a step until the men with the lights had made a complete sweep of the ground in front of us. The trench stretched ahead. There was no way to estimate its length. Radiation levels read normal. We continued.

I had a small recorder in my pack with a wire that ran up my sleeve to a microphone. I dictated our findings to this point.

We came upon a second piece of wreckage at 75 to 100 yards, then a third, a fourth. The sizes of the debris grew with their frequency. I had one of my men scan the perimeter with his light. No doubt we would find more scrap in the desert scrub. We marked the area with small yellow flags.

Another wave of the Geiger counter showed no radiation spikes coming from any of the objects.

I had dropped to one knee to get a closer look at the largest chunk we had found so far when one of the medics rushed by. I followed quickly.

If you are prone to human curiosity, you have already looked at the attached photos and know what I am about to write is true.

It was at about 150 yards, (my estimations could be questioned at this point and rightfully so) we found the first body part, a partial arm. The men worked as if they had done this a hundred times. Not one step of procedure was overlooked. The limb scanned negative for radiation. The medic produced a camera and photographed the arm from several angles like the forensic pathologist which he was. The soldier with the light followed his direction focusing the beam for optimal results.

The arm was humanoid and intact from where I guessed the elbow joint would have been. Whatever clothing or protective suit it had been wearing was seared and unrecognizable. The creature's skin color and texture were unknown due to burns and injury. We planted more flags to mark the find.

With one call, a dozen specialists with high level clearance would be summoned. A perimeter would be secured by regular troops who would be fed a cover story over and over until they actually believed it. Anyone who doubted what they were told would be shamed into obedience by having their patriotism questioned. If this wasn't enough, the soldier would be *reassigned*, in so many words.

I switched frequencies and ordered the two men back at the truck to start setting up the lighting, as we were going to be here for a while.

The darkness of the desert night still hid the length of the crevasse created by whatever had crashed here.

I have transcribed the remainder of this document from my recordings. My notes had become sporadic by this point and my memories of these fantastic events cannot be fully trusted.

While I tried to remain emotionless in front of the men, the voice on my tapes betrayed me. Quivers and stutters preceded every entry as I listed the details of the discoveries of more wreckage and body parts.

We found a pair of long beams curled at the front from the impact. They were metal (gold or gold colored) and engraved with unusual markings. Radiation levels still remained within safe parameters.

The scorched and broken leg of some unfortunate desert animal was found. Its hoof scraped the ground marking where the leg had been dragged before being torn from its body.

The call of one of my men was clear in the background of the recordings. "Medic, we have a live one here." His shout was followed by the trample of boots as we rushed to join him.

Our search and recovery continued for the next two days. We were joined by Colonel Conroy and a group of experts whose number and names I cannot recall. Every scrap of body or craft was carefully bagged, documented and loaded into a secure vehicle for transport to the base.

Doctors and scientists from every discipline would reconstruct and reverse-engineer our findings for months before delivering their official report. But my men and I knew what we had found.

We were debriefed and warned. Our freedom and professional lives dangled in front of us by men even we didn't believe existed. We were sold the weather balloon story, which was reinforced to the point of brainwashing. When I suggested we tell people the truth because no one would believe it, I earned a one-on-one with the colonel. He gave me a month off at an Army hospital to meet with doctors who would help me deal with the *stresses* of my job. More reprogramming was what it was, much longer than a month (five months from the night of the event to my return), but I played the "good" soldier and was eventually released. I rejoined my men. Most had shown better discipline than I and had gone along with the program. A couple of others were still absent, surely enjoying the same treatment I had received.

To my amazement, I found my notes and the recordings I have used to create this document, untouched in my locker. Among my other belongings I found a manila file someone planted, containing the photographs I referenced earlier. I leafed through them, confirming my sanity that the Army doctors had me questioning during my stay. Some of the pictures were from the recovery in the desert, others were on base. I recognized the interior of a building in one of the shots. The engineers must have been working around the clock to have recreated the image in the photo.

The colonel restored my command, and the men still respected my rank, but I could sense a discomfort among them. Did they know I had questioned the orders to forget what we had seen and swallow the cover story? Surely, they knew that's what had become of the other men who were no longer in their numbers. But the file of photos? Did the colonel have someone plant them so he could hide me away once and for all for insubordination? Or was there some other reason?

I shuffled through the pictures for the hundredth time, as I'm sure you have by now, still amazed each time at the images they showed. Again, I recognized the interior of a building in one of the shots and knew I had to see for myself.

I caught whiff of a rumor one day that the recovered craft and the remains of its crew (I never did find out the fate of the survivor we found) were being moved to a more secure location. Knowing how things work in the military, I estimated I had at least three days to figure a way into the hangar that had been transformed into a makeshift lab where the recovered craft was hidden. But this being a special case, I didn't want to risk missing what I knew would be my only chance to see what was inside.

I decided to go that night. I didn't have much of a plan, but my need was so strong I almost felt it was worth getting caught just to get a glimpse of the reconstructed wreckage. I had seen it in the pictures you are holding, but to be so close and not get a live look, well, my willpower was too weak. I had believed as a child, reasoned away that belief with logic as an adult, but now the truth was right there.

I gained access to the building with little trouble. The ease of my entrance had me thinking the craft might already have been moved under my nose, but I continued. It was dark and quiet inside; I risked a small flashlight, directing its beam at the floor.

Being a military building, the hallways were long and straight with lots of doors but few intersections. I turned left at a corridor I knew would lead to the largest open area in the hangar. I came to a set of double doors. They were chained and padlocked. The lack of guards or any activity at all made me nervous and had me believing the site had been abandoned after all. I pulled on the lock and found the chain had not even been laced through the door handles. It was open.

Had I been a thief, I may have realized I was walking into a trap. But I wasn't, and I didn't.

I played my flashlight toward the center of the room. It was there, what I had risked my career on to come see. Portable stairs were located on either end of a platform like a stage made for the most incredible show ever produced. My foot hit the first step.

A series of loud clicks echoed around the chamber. Glaring lights caught me mid-step. I heard the colonel address me.

"Was it worth it?" he asked.

I continued up the steps. I knew the game was over, but I wasn't in any danger. The colonel would let me have a good long look before a pair of MPs dragged me away for the last time.

He explained how I had been part of one of mankind's greatest discoveries. He went on about all the technology they had discovered;

communications, medical, and new energy sources, and how it could all be used to benefit humanity. He listed radar advancements and stealth capabilities on the military side of the ledger. He told how they were baffled at first as to why they had never tracked one of these crafts before. They thought they would find some sort of cloaking device, but it turned out to be a special non-reflective paint that rendered the craft invisible to traditional detection methods.

I looked at the object on the platform. Gleaming red with blinding gold rails and trim. Graceful curves, high in the rear, tapered toward the front. Overstuffed burgundy leather with brass rivets the size of quarters stretched to form seats in front of a tiny instrument cluster with candy-striped controls.

I thought of my childhood. I thought of children around the world. I thought of their innocence.

The ultimate symbol of their purity lay in front of me.

It was a sleigh.

Santa's sleigh

When I woke the next day, to my surprise, I found I was in my barracks and not some grey cell buried deep in a mountain. I recalled a compromise the colonel and I had settled on. I immediately set about creating this memoir. I mailed it to a safe place, as my insurance policy against the colonel should he decide to go back on our agreement. I later sent this addendum to further explain the outcome of these events.

Colonel Conroy disclosed everything. The sleigh had been on a training flight. The bodies, elves. The leg and hoof, reindeer. They had since learned how to track the numerous sleighs that made flights to and from several locations around the globe. They did not interfere, but they monitored. The president himself had decided to notify all the governments of the world of the discovery (although I doubt he shared everything) and the need for it to remain secret at all costs. They unanimously agreed.

Instead of being sent to the stockade, the colonel left me in charge of my team. We had new orders, however. We were part of a larger group of which there were many. We would be on stand-by once a year (I'll let you guess what night) with large military aircraft filled with gifts.

Our mission was to monitor the sleigh deliveries and be ready to complete their rounds should there be another unfortunate accident.

Every military in the world did the same.

For one night a year, mankind put their differences aside and came together to ensure the wishes of Earth's children would come true.

# About the Author

Chris Blinn lives in Marshfield MA, with his wife and three sons. He has worked for the Massachusetts Bay Transportation Authority for the past 24 years in different roles. Sci-fi writing and reading top his list of hobbies as well as fishing and hockey. His most recent work, "The job that ate my brain," was included in 4 Horsemen's *Paranormal Incorporated: The Offices of Supernatural Being* anthology. Other stories can be found in *Demonic Medicine* anthology and the Original *Toilet Zone* anthology. Self-published works include the novellas *Stealing Stanley,* a comedy action story and *Lane 10,* a coming-of-age story with a paranormal twist as well as *Madison X,* a sci-fi novel. All are available on Amazon.com.

# Memo to All Attendees

by
Sheila Hartney

# Memo to All Attendees

From: Plvren32z4, Head of Conference Planning

To: All attendees at recent event on third planet of star system YGR95-17

Subject: Just a few people can spoil it for the rest of us.

It looks as though this is one planet we won't be going back to any time soon. A joke is a joke, but still. You need to think things through. Yes, you do.

I get it. I know it seemed like a good idea to hold the latest NewPlanetCon here. It was a new planet for us, and it looked like a good choice. Plus, we did choose a relatively unpopulated location on this planet.

I'm sure you all had fun, but you really should have been thinking about the consequences. Okay, so it was the middle of summer in a hot and dry place, but everyone ought to know by now that no matter what planet we go to, the local intoxicants are almost always stronger than what most of us are used to. And this planet? Well, they have a galaxy-wide reputation here.

We all like a good Lost Spaceman party after these things. Yes, it's a long-standing tradition. But whose idea was it to dump one of our ships, complete with the space traveler prototype models? I'm looking at you, Roykin.

I've been informed that the locals use primitive balloons to track their weather, and we're trying to put out that what they found was nothing more than one of their weather balloons. Let's just hope they buy it.

The High Council has suggested we hire the sign-makers from ADR47 and have them start posting signs everywhere warning others in the Federation that they need to stay away. I'm told that we can consider putting the signs in their cultivated fields.

Ensure that the sign-makers, the ones who post on those fields, get out the message that this planet is off-limits for at least a hundred of their sun-cycles. That should be long enough for them to forget this incident.

Yes, I know the locals will probably start mimicking them, but we can't do anything to prevent that.

Meanwhile, plans are going forward for our next NewPlanetCon on the 5th planet of star system SLO43, which is much closer to the center of the galaxy than we're used to, so be aware there will be radiation-suit requirements for this one. See you there!

# About the Author

Sheila Hartney lives in New Mexico, Land of Enchantment, with gloriously clear skies and vast numbers of science fiction writers, many of whom she counts as friends. Many years ago, she was a Writer of the Future and, more recently, she attended the Taos Toolbox to hone her writing skills. More than one trip to Roswell helped inspire this anthology.

# The Plaintive King
by
J. Edward Gregal

# The Plaintive King

Okay, Dennis, I just dropped the link in the chat. You want to watch the video and tell the listeners what you're seeing?"

"Sure! Starting now. Looks like a river, a flood. It's moving really fast. You can see some trees sticking up out of the water, other trees floating by. Camera is tracking something pink, kind of pale. Splayed out, not moving at all. Really blurry. Zooming in…is that a body? It's hard to— *holy shit*."

Christine laughs. "Pause here. Dude, it's bananas, right?"

"That was a hand, emerging from the water behind the first shape. Same pink as the first floating thing. How many fingers? Didn't look like enough."

"I watched a forty-five-minute breakdown of the footage last night in preparation—"

*"Jesus."*

"Yeah, well, just trying to be thorough for our beloved Strangenessers!"

"That name's not going to work no matter how hard you push, Chris."

She waits a beat before speaking again.

"*Anyway*, in the analysis it seems pretty clear that we're looking at a hand—with an opposable thumb—and three fingers. And not, like, your standard human hand missing a digit. We get a very clear look just as the video cuts off, it's three evenly spaced fingers."

"Whaaaaaa?"

"Dude, I know. Keep going!"

"Okay, ummm…video stops just as we see, well, uh, *that*. It's back, zoomed in and looking farther down the river. Just the rapids or whatever you call it. The guy shooting the video is just saying 'holy shit' over and over. 'Oh god, I hope I got it, I hope I got the face, holy shit, holy shit,' et cetera. A face?"

"There's the bummer. The guy who shot it—fellow Jackson resident, *woot woot!*—says he was trying to capture the first shape and didn't notice the hand pop up right away, so he stopped the video. Just as he did that, he says he saw *a face*."

"…and of course, he didn't catch it in time."

"Nope, classic."

"Convenient is what it is."

"Sure, you can look at it like that, but I think there's something more to it. This is a classic element of high strangeness. Witnesses experience something, but for some reason the experience is confined to them and only them. No matter what, it stays subjective. One perspective—John Keel talked about this at length—is that it's intentional. The phenomena are fucking with us. Somebody, some*thing* is pulling the strings. It's the Ultraterrestrials, dude."

"So, you're saying those were Ultraterrestrials in the river? Crab King is an Ultraterrestrial?"

"No! Well, I don't know. And as an aside, Crab *King* feels like a misnomer, there's clearly at least two of them.

"But maybe these...*crab people*...are from another dimension—you know Jacques Vallée and the whole interdimensional hypothesis we talked about a few episodes back? Maybe the Ultraterrestrials stranded them here from another world, maybe they're fucking with them just as much as they're fucking with us. They're cosmic tricksters, so why would the phenomenon be restricted to humans?"

"You think that, really?"

"I don't know. It's all speculative. But things have definitely been happening here. Strange lights have been reported in this region for centuries. And lights are classically a harbinger of other, weirder things. The first Crab King sighting was in April 2020, by that hiker up on Mount Pleasant. A week later, there's the hiker who came down the mountain with klieg conjunctivitis and an hour of missing time. Classic shit, classic. And then that hunter's footage from last November we talked about—"

"Which sucked."

"Yeah, admittedly it wasn't the best. But still, we saw something bipedal and pink step out of the river and into the thicket. But you have to admit the footage he got of the footprints—" Dennis groans and Christine sighs before resuming. "The footprints are really clear in that footage, and you can see they have three toes!"

"So, all these purported sightings—"

Christine keeps an eye on the dark road ahead of her as she stops the podcast. Dennis's plosives rattled her car's speakers, she'll have to go back and fix them before they drop the episode tomorrow night. Again. It feels like a trivial thing, but the listener numbers have been up and internet fascination with the Crab King has spiked since that video dropped. With half of Medium Strangeness based out of Jackson, they have a unique personal link to the story. This might be the episode that gets them actual sponsors. With a little Squarespace money, she might be able to get her degree without having to pick up shifts at Pancake Yurt to get by.

She pulls up behind Miranda's car and triggers the motion-activated floodlight by the front steps. Meredith will be here already, of course; she's always the first to show up.

"Shit," she says, glancing at her phone and realizing it's already 9:20. Mary's usually next, so she's likely inside, too. They're probably sitting around the table in front of their character sheets discussing whether they should kick her out of the group for being such a habitually-late fuck-up.

She smiles and grabs her dice bag. No way. How many times has her Sleep spell saved their ass in this campaign? And who figured out, much to K's consternation, they could defeat that entire village of zombie miners, without losing a single hit point, with a stealthy daytime assassination of their parasitic wasp queen? Nah, the Sparagmos Company need Ymanie the magic user if they're ever going to keep the Tears of Vummor from the hands of Elizabeth the Necromancer, Worm Queen of Krual-Goi. Without her, the dead would rise and sweep the multiverse, and then what else would they do on Thursday nights? Play that cyberpunk game Mary's been threatening to run for the last two years? Mary is good, but nobody can run a game like K.

She gets out of the car, locks it, and looks around. There's just K's house, the road behind her, and trees, nothing but trees. And darkness. And whatever is surely lurking in that darkness, watching her. The fine hair stands up on her neck and she stifles the urge to get back in her car, go home, and fix Dennis's plosives.

This place never ceases to creep her out. Sure, K pays only half what Christine does in rent, but the downside is that she lives in a haunted fucking forest.

Once the goosebumps go down, she breathes in the cool, clean night air and admits the sound of crickets—and only crickets—is actually pretty nice. Her apartment is sandwiched between Piano Man, the retired concert pianist who isn't retired enough to stop him from playing nine hours a day, and that couple locked in a daily cycle of catastrophic breakups and full volume make up sex. If she lived out here, Medium Strangeness Studios South could go from a hastily assembled blanket fort in her bedroom closet to a permanent space in her house.

She looks around again. There's the risk she'll get dragged off into the woods by crawlers, but maybe tomorrow she'll look for a place here just outside of town anyway.

As she walks toward the house, Miranda's "I BRAKE FOR P-ZOMBIES" bumper sticker confounds her, again, and she decides this time she's not going to forget to ask what it means when she gets inside.

All bumper sticker thoughts halt when she sees the slime.

Spread across the pavers by the front step is about a half-gallon of some purplish…stuff. She kneels, careful to avoid putting a knee in it, takes out her phone, and turns on the light. It's translucent, a dark purple, streaked with strands of an opaque white. A large splash is concentrated here, but more trails off into the overgrown grass to the right.

A crooked grin spreads across her face. She knows what this is. Back when she first asked her best friend to do Medium Strangeness, the paranormal podcast market was already pretty saturated. She'd listened to at least an episode of every one she could find, ranging from well-produced shows backed by big media networks and hosted by B-list celebrities, down to the ones with the audio quality of two speaker phones recorded by another phone in a wind tunnel, shows with hosts so aggressively inept the finished result was almost outsider art. With all these shows churning out weekly episodes, there were few topics left untouched. The Kelly-Hopkinsville Goblins, the Dover Demon, even The Sandown Clown had hours and hours' worth of discussion readily available for consumption. She wanted to kick off the show with something nobody else had discussed yet, and after perusing her cherished paranormal library of 1970's paranormal mass market paperbacks, vanity press delirium, and heavy hitters from the likes of Fort, Keel, Coleman, and Vallée—the core of which were posthumous gifts from her late, great, Uncle Danny, a true devotee of all things Fortean—she found a topic that rode the line of obscure enough that she couldn't find a podcast episode devoted to it and interesting enough to make her stay up until 4 a.m. doing research.

"Star jelly," she whispers.

There are records, going back to the 1800s, of individuals finding strange, gelatinous substances in their yards, often in the wake of meteor showers. It's often whitish grey, sometimes it glows, but in many cases it's purple. Just like this.

As she gets on her hands and knees the smell, like ammonia, is strong enough to make her light-headed.

What the fuck is this stuff? She lifts an exploratory finger and then thinks better of it.

The star jelly phenomenon inspired the movie *The Blob*, and one of the main takeaways from that film, above all else, is you don't touch the space slime with your bare hands.

Hopefully K has some rubber gloves inside.

She stands, brushes dirt off her knees, and walks up the stairs. She knocks three times before opening the door.

"Hey, sorry I'm late, podcast stuff! Also did you know you have star jelly…"

No one is at the table. K's hand-painted GM screen is up, depicting their group battling the Grue in its storm of swirling darkness. The character sheets are untouched in their folder and the table is otherwise empty. A few steps closer and she sees an Armored Mastiff Comics tote bag on the floor next to Miranda's usual seat.

"K?"

Christine drops her bag on the table and looks around the cluttered living room. She pauses in front of the antique mirror and sees K's geriatric tabby Dora coolly watching from the cat tower in the reflection behind her. Christine turns and approaches her with an outstretched hand, but three rapid-fire tail twitches tell her maybe she should try again another night.

On the coffee table, a nearly spent stick of incense burns in a ceramic holder on a stack of battered large-format fine art books. Sandalwood? Was this one sandalwood? All incense smells the same to her. Stinky.

"Hey, K? Guys?"

Dora voices her disapproval with a whiny growl more cute than threatening. Christine smiles.

A faint "Oh," comes from the studio. The door is partially open, streaked up and down with a Jackson Pollock gestalt of K's fingerprints in paint.

She pushes open the door and finds K sitting at a 4 by 3 canvas. She looks up at Christine briefly before shifting back to the painting. Her brush strokes are fast, almost frantic. The sclera of her eyes are a mottled pink and red. Tears run down her cheeks.

"Dude, what's up? Are you okay? Your eyes…"

K nods, holds up a finger, deftly paints three more lines, and puts the brush down. She takes a deep breath, uses the back of her hand to push her hair from the closely cropped right side of her head, and studies her work for a moment. Then she shifts her attention to Christine.

"Hey. Sorry." Her deep voice is hoarse, like she just woke up.

"First of all, what's going on with your eyes? And second, where is everybody?"

K looks down at the cracked screen of her phone and tilts her head.

"Uhh, last night that gallery called to officially offer me that show."
She nods, blinking a few times before looking up at her painting.

"Oh shit, congrats!"

K nods. "Thanks. I, uhh, guess I cracked open a bottle of wine to
celebrate while I finished that Vummor piece." She gestures toward the
corner.

Christine approaches and looks. Like all of K's work, it's breathtaking.
It depicts a scarred man in plate mail kneeling beside a thin, lifeless woman
in bed. Tears stream down his face, cutting tracks through grime. It's
always a trip to see how well K's depiction of their campaign's historical
events jive so well with the way she describes them to the group, but then
again, she's always been one of those prodigies who excels at most things
she does.

"Got a bit hammered, and I guess I got some varnish in my eyes.
Wasn't so bad this morning, but it's way worse now." She raises her palm
to her right eye.

"You sure that's from varnish? Would it get better and then worse
like that?"

K shrugs.

"Dude, it looks bad. Maybe we should get you over to urgent care or
something? I mean, it's your eyes, you need those!" K nods in silence,
wipes her hands on her stained work pants.

"Where is everybody anyway?" Christine asks.

K looks down at her phone again. "Not here yet I guess?"

"Meredith and Miranda's cars are out front. Mary should be here too,
she usually puts her bike around back, right?"

K nods again, eyes flitting back to the canvas.

Christine comes around behind her and looks at what she's been
painting. K's finished works are typically vibrant and colorful, mostly
depictions of some kind of action scene in a fantasy setting. Christine
doesn't usually see K's work in the early stages—she is very particular
about the way she works—so it's fascinating to see what she has down
now.

This feels so very different from her typical work, expressionist and
warped somehow. Rudimentary brush slashes delimit the exteriors of an
architecture like a jagged migraine aura, all sharp points and acute angles.
The only objects not composed of straight lines are two celestial objects
placed in the otherwise featureless white sky, presumably moons. One is
bisected by a two-pronged tower on the far horizon. It's already one of the

most evocative things K's done to date, even at this early stage. What could even live in a city like this?

It takes Christine a moment to pull her eyes away from the painting and remember what she was doing. K is already picking up her brush again.

"So, uh, I guess I'll check the backyard real quick, but maybe you should clean up a little, I think we need to get you looked at right away. Okay?" She touches K's shoulder, who stops and glances back at Christine. God, her eyes look grisly.

"Yeah, that's probably smart," K says. It sounds like someone is playing her voice back at three-quarter speed. K drank a little too much sometimes, got stoned occasionally, but historically never touched anything else save what she consumes during what she calls her "yearly psychedelic recalibration." Christine can't help but wonder if she's been messing with something harder tonight.

"Get ready. I'm going to see where everyone went." Christine walks back out through the living room and into the kitchen. Light shines through the dust and grime of the window over the sink. There's a motion-activated light in the backyard too, so they must be out there. When her hand touches the cool doorknob, she shivers as a passing thought comes— *What if it's not them out there?*—that's quickly dispelled as she opens the door.

Mary's bike is on the ground a few feet away. Her bag is still in the front basket, affixed with a bungee net.

Christine steps outside. The air is cooler out here by far, but that star jelly ammonia smell is stronger. The light extends maybe 20 feet or so to the roughly square border of the treeline. To her left is a set of rusty patio furniture and an even rustier grill. The shed lurks off in the far-right corner, trees climbing up a steep hill into the darkness beyond it.

"Hey guys?"

There's a sound, a rustling, somewhere off to the right. Goosebumps break out across her forearms because the cricket chirps are gone, silent, replaced with a heavy, threatening stillness. The thudding of her heart is all she can hear. She knows what this is, never thought she'd actually experience it. This was some Oz Factor shit, and although she's always wished to experience the strange, the liminal, now that she stands here in silence, half-choking on star jelly fumes, she wants to turn around and go, get out, never look back.

She looks, sees nothing beyond the half circle of light. She picks out something in the grass nearby, screws up her courage and takes a few steps toward it. The smell is overpowering now.

A u-lock. The rubber at one end of the crossbar is torn. She picks it up and it glistens purple in the light. She drops it and something moves in the gloom by the shed.

"Mary?"

She hopes it's Mary, but her every instinct tells her it's not. But still, she stalks though the ankle high weeds toward it.

In the dark, on the side of the shed, her three friends lie side by side, a few feet apart, on the hill. They are laid out with their feet pointing up toward the slope, equidistant, posed exactly the same. Their disfigured heads are at the base. Shallow channels in the dirt beneath them direct the blood to the level ground just to their left. The blood flows under an inert, whitish-pink humanoid form. Its body is composed of overlapping plates, and its shadowed eyes stare pale blue at the sky above.

A similar shape stands in the shadows. It steps closer and Christine can see it holds a bright-pink hand to a large crack in its chest plate. A purple ichor flows out between its three fingers. The ammonia smell overpowers her, there is a flash of blue light, and then it is over.

Inside, K stands up to get ready, but the scene on the canvas draws her back in. She picks up her brush and goes back to painting. When Christine comes back in, she can stop. It's close. She can fill in the details later, but she's almost there.

She focuses on a tiny structure at the very edge of the painting that's like a haphazard stack of interlocking black hexagrams. As she works on this building, she hears it—this often happens when she's deeply immersed in her work—and it's like rushing air over a slow, steady grinding sound, like huge stone wheels spinning against one another deep in the earth.

She barely hears the back door open. Dora hisses in the living room and bolts into her hiding spot under a cabinet here in the studio. It is almost enough to make her look up, but the near subsonic grinding keeps her locked into her work. Someone enters the room and something sharp cuts through the accustomed smell of her paint, but she can't look up. The building is complete, but there's one last thing. Two last things. It takes all her skill to convey the two figures at the edge of this massive city, a city she now understands is dead, but she's got the skill to do it. When she paints the last figure she sobs, she knows they're dead too, lost. She sets the brush down and looks back over her shoulder.

The pink man, sharp and armored, stares with solid cobalt-blue eyes, not at her, but at the canvas in front of her. The grinding sound in her head keeps her lulled, passive, as she stares at it. The creature is far from human, very far from it, but the way it tilts its head makes her think it's really studying the work somehow.

"I'm sorry," she whispers. "I'm so sorry." The grinding sound comes to an abrupt halt, and she screams. It's on her then.

Hours later, the backyard light clicks on. The pink shape staggers away, alone, from the inert bodies it had so carefully arranged. The leaking in its carapace has finally slowed, but it still presses its hand to the crack as it lopes across the yard. It enters the kitchen and walks back to the studio.

Dora's face peers out, eyes wide, from beneath the cabinet. The creature looks at the cat for a few moments and then returns to the canvas. It stands, inert, for some time, touches one of the tiny figures, smearing it, and then lashes out at the painting, knocking it off the easel. The cat bolts out of the room.

The thing moves into the hall, leaving a purple, sticky impression of its three-fingered hand on the door over K's own handprint in dried white paint. It moves in front of the mirror. The glow starts on its chest, spreads up the neck, across the flat cheeks, and its eyes brighten in an arc flash. It does this over and over, but no matter how many times it tries, it can't forget.

# About the Author

J Edward Gregal lives in the Pacific Northwest with his ever-patient partner and their ever-insistent cats. He spends his time there riding and working on bicycles, crying to "Caught In the Middle" by Dio, and navigating the futile landscape of late capitalism with exhausted volition.

He can be reached at jedwardgregallovescats@gmail.com

# The Purple
## by
## Dana Bell

# The Purple

**F**ound the car on the side of the road," the store owner told Bob Smith, and shoved a picture across the wooden counter. "Found the young fella's camera near the cliff path."

Smith, a long-time paranormal investigator, nodded as he studied the picture. "Missing persons' report says they never located the couple." He'd done his homework in Denver. The woman's face, Edna, haunted him. Young, pretty with a rare innocence. Her boyfriend had been average-looking.

He'd thought about them while taking the mountain highway after he'd left Denver. Luckily, he'd seen the turnoff for Red Cliff, a small town a few miles beyond his destination,

"Never did," the owner responded, pulling Bob's mind back to the moment. The owner, a balding man who reminded him of a TV character on a show his mother had loved, nervously shoved his hands into his pockets. "They weren't the first to disappear."

He'd learned that, too. There had been a number of odd disappearances since the town's last residents had moved out in 1985. Bob rubbed his neck, thinking his brown hair needed to be cut. He'd make an appointment in a few days.

"They finish the clean up?" Bob already knew the answer. He wanted to hear a local's opinion.

"Think so. Land has changed hands a few times and there'd been plans to build a resort." He didn't miss the wistful tone. "Fell through."

From what Bob noticed, the area was poor with few jobs. Older homes and scattered businesses just scraping by. A resort would have brought in tourists and badly-needed income.

"Of course," the owner continued. "If they fell in the river, might never find their bodies." The man shuddered. "Long way down, and the mine flooded years back."

"Understand there was a caretaker." He waited.

"Odd thing, that. Caretaker vanished when the land got sold. No one has seen him since."

"He didn't live here?"

"Nope. Not in Leadville, either. No one knows much about him."

He made a mental note. Another aspect to investigate. "Think the owners would mind if I snooped around?"

"Gate is probably locked."

Bob smiled. A locked gate wasn't an obstacle. "I'll keep that in mind."

"You be careful. Hate to add you to the list."

"Me, too." He left the store, but not before noticing several empty shelves and the lack of paying customers. Told him all he needed to know about the current economy.

Outside, he paused. With the altitude it was difficult to catch his breath.

He crawled into his rented four-wheel drive and headed back down the road to Gilman. Driving more slowly than he liked, he knew he had to be careful. Sharp turns and speeding could end his trip before it had even begun. He had no desire to be lost in a ravine or swept away in the river.

The ghost town appeared, trees lining the road and a sharp turnoff toward the entrance. He parked and gazed at the once-thriving mining town. Shuttered houses stood looking over the deserted town. He could see the remnants of the original businesses and school. Swings moved back and forth. Bob shivered, pulling his coat tighter. Cold up here still, even in June.

Walking the graveled road to the gate, he looked around. Abandoned. Left to rot. A reminder of a glory age long gone. When silver had been King, before the crash and other valued minerals dwindled away.

After waiting several minutes, no one challenged him. He climbed the gate and landed on the other side with a thump. Deep grooves indicated large trucks had been there recently. Probably the cleanup crews.

Walking down the dirt road and into the desolate town, he took out his phone, using the camera to take several pictures. He could tell why the property was desirable. Attached to the mountain on one side, the other three sides ended in sharp cliffs, all of which reached down to the raging river below. If the couple he sought had fallen for any reason, like trying to reach the mine, their bodies might never be discovered.

He heard a scratch and looked at a store front window. A face appeared and just as quickly disappeared. Stepping inside the open door, he saw no movement. No evidence anyone had been there since the town shut down.

What caught his eye was the purple fungus growing along the window. It wasn't like any he'd seen before. Bright, goopy, and probably harmless since it hadn't been cleaned out. He touched it, rubbing it between his fingers, a tingle running through him. Wiping it on his jeans, he shrugged and left, walking along the cracked sidewalks, plants struggling through the cracks. He gazed in the windows or open doors. No contents had been left behind. On occasion he'd see a face, which vanished before he could clearly focus on it.

Ghosts of the past, no doubt, stuck between worlds and unable to escape. He'd seen such before. If the town was ever destroyed, where would they go?

Bob found the school. Faintly, he heard laughter and saw children's shadows playing on swings. A woman rang a bell, the sound drifting on the cold breeze. Youngsters ran to her, their voices and laughter echoing.

Singing reached his ears as the miners walked to work, each disappearing over the cliff.

'Mine is under water,' echoed in his mind.

Taking a street heading back the way he'd come, he stopped. The woman from the picture he'd seen in Denver, the one who'd stirred his curiosity stood there. She shook her head, her expression becoming alarmed before her form shimmered into nothingness.

"So, you died here," he said quietly. "I'm sorry." Sadness filled him. Such a waste.

His quest had ended with Edna's demise. He knew her fate and had no reason to linger. He trudged along. From the road above came a crashing sound. Through the pines, whose scent filled the air, a car appeared, its journey ending as it struck one of the houses.

Thinking someone might be hurt, he hurried toward the wreck.

"Happened years ago. You can't help."

He pivoted, staring at an old man dressed like a cowboy, a gun belt slung across his middle. "You're one of us now."

"Excuse me?" Fear shot through him.

"Dang fools didn't clean it all up. Didn't think it was harmful."

All around Bob people gathered, each wearing clothes from many time periods. Ghosts he had encountered before, and he wasn't afraid. This…this was different, and he felt ice fingers crawling along his spine.

He took a step backward, his heart pounding, making him dizzy due to the thin air.

"The mines released something they couldn't control," the old timer continued. "By the time they'd realized, was too late."

"What do you mean?"

"I'm not no scientist, but best we know, it creates a twilight world and traps folks." He pointed to the road above as a semi drove past. "They go about their lives and never see us."

"I investigate ghosts." Had to be the only explanation.

"We ain't ghosts." The man leaned closer. Bob could smell whiskey. "Never died."

"What does this?" He backed up. Not happening, his mind told him.

"The purple. You touched it."

Staring at his hand he remembered the odd tingling afterward.

"Them who disappeared come here. Folks like you think we're ghosts."

Madness. Bob shook his head denying what he heard. "I'm leaving." He pushed past the cowboy.

"You can try."

He had to escape. He had to. Climbing the gate, he ran to his car and inserted the key. It went right through without touching the lock. Again he tried, and again.

"You can't leave," a gentle voice told him. "Come." Edna extended her hand. She was dressed in jeans and a sweater. "It's not so bad."

He stared into her face. "What happened to your boyfriend?"

She gave him a knowing look. "He got what was coming to him. Hope he enjoyed his swim."

"You killed him." Horror filled him. He couldn't believe this woman capable of murder.

"No." Her eyes took on a distant look. "He tried to find me and couldn't. In the end he tried to get back to the mine and fell."

"I'm sorry." He had no idea what else to say.

"I'm not. He bullied me." She extended her hand again. "Come."

Taking her cold hand, Bob took one final look at his car, knowing his name would be added to the strange disappearances in Gilman, Colorado. A fitting end to his unusual career.

With a smile, he accepted his fate and joined the other ghosts. His only regret: not getting to write his article and share his findings with his colleagues.

# About the Author

Dana Bell is a Colorado author who enjoys setting stories in places she's either lived or visited. Her cats, who have decided they own her, have inspired many of her tales, particularly her cat vampire series and the post-apocalyptic Winter trilogy. *Winter Awakening* is the first book. The second, *Winter Emergence,* is soon to be released.

*God's Gift* is the prequel book to both the Winter trilogy and the soon to be released *Homefall Search,* 2024, the first in a new trilogy set in the Five Systems and Borders universe. *Bast's Chosen Ones and other Cat Adventures* contain many feline short works, including the cat vampires.

She also writes Paranormal Romance under the pseudonym Belle Blukat. Her first book *Blood Bride* is currently available. There are also some short reads on Amazon.

As an editor, she has lost track of how many anthologies she's edited and how many writers' careers she has launched. As she says, she's a proud mama of all her babes.

She's an award-winning poet of nature poems and was nominated for the Rhysling award for Speculative poetry.

Her hobbies include designing flower arrangements, building, decorating, and making up stories about her dollhouses, and using clay pots to make candle holders. She has lived in five states, traveled over half the US, including a cruise to the Bahamas, and hopes one day to shop at Diagon Alley.

# Aliens Squashed My Cousin

by
Michael W. Clark

# Aliens Squashed My Cousin

quashed?" Sheriff Grace Willisburg looked down at the large, flattened mess on the two-lane paved road. "You think it's human?"

"Human?" The short old man pointed. "That's my cousin, Jesse, Jesse Pimbolt!" The old guy scratched his thin, blue-jeaned butt. "Human may be saying too much about him."

"You are reporting a hit and run, then." The sheriff took off her hat, placing it upside down on her black and white cruiser hood. She was hot from the long, slow drive up. She pulled out her hand-held computer. "How long ago?"

"Last night." The old man shook his head. "But ain't no hit and run, well, at least, no car."

"Yeah, this sort of injury? Has to be really big. A lumber truck?"

The old man quivered while nodding and then shook his head. "Bigger'n that. Much bigger."

"Earth moving equipment would have dug up the road." The sheriff thought this was just another example of crazy old white men on drugs, COWMOD. Cow-mad. The northern part of Washington was full of them.

"Bigger'n that." The old man shook all over.

"What is bigger than an earth mover, a battleship? Aircraft carrier maybe?" She needed to be calmer. Pearly McBride was always telling her to stay calm, especially with the COWM.

"Craft alright, but a spaceship." The old man looked down and then looked up. "No ocean ship."

The sheriff automatically looked to the sky, too, but then jerked her head back down. "Your cousin was squashed by aliens? Oh, shit!" The sheriff sighed. "*Washingtonians must go nuts from boredom,*" the sheriff thought. "Sure it wasn't Bigfoot?"

"Think I'm crazy? Bigfoot's just tourist bullshit." The old man pointed down again. "Aliens squashed my cousin."

"Where is the mega-vulture when you need it?" the sheriff muttered. A Seattle biotech firm did have a prehistoric mega-vulture. It got out last year, for a while. She had searched for it. They had a number of resuscitated extinct species, it later turned out. If they could get enough DNA from fossil bones, they could resurrect extinct organisms. *Making extinction extinct* was one of their marketing slogans. "Maybe it was the pygmy mammoth?" The sheriff still had to find out if this roadkill was human and then which specific human. The DNA from this roadkill would do it, too. Maybe they could resurrect this squashed cousin.

"Nah. Seen that thing down in Seattle. Looked like a fat, hairy pony. Squash your foot maybe. Aliens! Nothin' else it could be but aliens. Nah. Aliens squashed my cousin."

"That's the newspaper headline you're out for?" The sheriff sighed again. *Pearly will love this COWMOD*, she thought.

"Don't read media anymore. All lies." The old man scratched his butt again.

"You saw these aliens, I assume?" The sheriff typed into her hand-held. "Or their UFO?"

The old man shook his head. He put his right index finger near his right temple. "Heard 'em in here." He smiled and then grimaced. "Heard the crunching too." The old man shivered. "Skull poppin'."

"Why didn't you see anything if you heard things?" The sheriff had her own answer. *COWMOD!*

"It was dark." The old man burped. "You think I'm a whacko."

"It is one of many options which remain open." The sheriff pointed at the mess. "Can you show me any anything here to identify this as your cousin?"

"Hairs the same color." The old man pointed.

"Anything else?" The sheriff reached for her mobile phone. She was too far away for the radio to work.

The old man shook his head.

"Sure! We can do a DNA family typing." The sheriff looked at her watch. Her dinner with Pearly just went extinct. This potential crime scene would take excessive time.

"Aliens squashed my dog!" Frankie hung around the Sheriff's Office instead of going to school. Frankie always flunked his classes, whether he was there or not, so the teachers preferred him to go anywhere else but school. The Sheriff's Office was as good a place as any. It was the safest place in town.

The sheriff sighed.

Deputy Sheriff Eric laughed. "Aliens were driving a Buick, were they, Frankie?"

"He meant illegal aliens, didn't you, Frankie," Deputy Sheriff Elisabeth Gant countered.

"Don't know." Frankie stuttered. "Maybe?"

"Well, Frankie, could you go for a walk?" The sheriff was feeling extremely frustrated with all the side issues that came with the job in this county. Solving and preventing crime was less and less a part of her daily routine.

She forced a smile in Frankie's direction. "Please. I need to concentrate now." Public relations were dominating her daily routine. She was beginning to hate the public because of these relations.

"Okay, Sheriff Willisburg." Frankie smiled broadly, grabbing his hat and jacket as he left.

"Fish are smarter." Eric said. Elisabeth smacked him.

"Thank you, Elisabeth." The sheriff glared at Eric. "Just to think, you used to be a regular guy."

Elisabeth shook her head. "He's been hanging with those other guys down at the Inn. Getting all macho, drunk, and loud."

Eric rubbed his cheek. "It's hard working for women."

"No, it's not." Elisabeth sighed.

"Just hard working for anyone." The sheriff sighed too.

"Monthly stuff makes a man crazy." Eric frowned instead of sighing.

"You had better go," Elisabeth whispered.

Eric blinked. He blinked again. Elisabeth flicked her finger for him to leave. The sheriff's breathing became heavier. Eric's face reddened. "I, ah, will go help Frankie find something to do. Maybe walk his squashed dog?" He grabbed his cap and jacket as he went out the door.

The sheriff didn't say anything.

"Jesse Pimbolt. The remains were, ah…are." Elisabeth read the report. "It was the old guy Jefferson's cousin, alright."

"He had one thing correct." The sheriff tapped her desk with the telescoping baton.

"Jesse wasn't the nicest of people though: burglary, vehicle theft, possession of stolen property. Non-violent felonies."

"Squashed felon." The sheriff said flatly. "Squashing is not a usual method of settling felon disputes." The sheriff frowned as Elisabeth giggled. "Aliens don't usually retaliate by squashing."

"Lasers and disrupters. Disintegration is more their style." Elisabeth added to the silliness.

"Like we would know what aliens do." The sheriff sighed. "Just weird. Maybe an angel stomped on him for being bad?" The sheriff tapped hardier. "Or being ugly? Never piss off an angel."

Elisabeth remained quiet. It was her best option.

"Damn this weird shit." The sheriff reached into the desk drawer and grabbed a tampon. "Don't say a word," she threatened as she walked to the ladies' room.

Elisabeth just shook her head. "Good thing Eric's out playing dog Frisbee."

Pearly and the sheriff sat naked in the hot tub. Pearly was drinking a colorful martini. The sheriff drank nothing.

"You do get annoyed easily at these times." Pearly sipped and smiled. Sipped and smiled. "I am your lawyer too. Such annoyance could make me have to charge you court appearance fees. Best not to waste money. Well, that is my legal opinion."

"Stupid annoys me. Aliens squashing people annoys me no matter the time of the month." The sheriff pulled back her wet hair.

"At least it's not the devil doing the squashing."

"Guess that is something." The sheriff nodded.

"Not Bigfoot either?"

The sheriff shook her head. "Not a big enough foot for this." It made her laugh. Pearly laughed, too.

"Does size matter?" Pearly giggled.

"In a human squashing? I think it does." The sheriff laughed harder.

"Aliens squashed my ATM machine?" The sheriff rubbed her nose with the palm of her right hand.

"Actually, the M stands for machine already, so it's just ATM," Eric stated. "Or AT machine."

The sheriff just glared at him. "Aliens need some petty cash. Where are they headed, Las Vegas?"

"Who else could squash stuff like this," Elisabeth cautiously pointed at the pictures of the flattened ATM at a highway off-ramp gas station.

"We have a mega-vulture in Seattle," the sheriff said. "A pygmy mammoth, too."

"So, some hi-tech company has created an alien?" Eric pointed to the mountains.

The sheriff rubbed her nose again.

Elisabeth intruded. "Tech. Alien-like tech. Right, Sheriff?"

"Seems more logical than an alien squash squad."

"Pimbolt was a burglary-type felon," Eric ventured.

"See how easy this actually is?" The sheriff put her hands on the desk. "Check for break-ins at high tech firms."

"And Pimbolt's known associates," Eric pointed his index finger in the air.

"Been reading, too, I see," the sheriff said to Elisabeth but looked at Eric.

"A little knowledge and danger thingy?" Elisabeth looked at Eric also.

"Exactly!" The sheriff chuckled.

"Standing right here!" Eric replied.

"And why is that? Get to work," the sheriff snapped.

The sheriff and Eric stood outside an obviously hand-built cabin, a very old hand-built cabin.

"Pimbolt's known associate lives here?" Eric stood beside the Sheriff's Department Land Rover 4x4 vehicle. *All-situations vehicle*, the previous sheriff had called them. "Well, if you call being in there living. Looks more like punishment to me."

"Now, now, Eric. Be open to everyone's lifestyle choices." The sheriff stood beside her cruiser. It had been her first purchase as Sheriff.

Eric chuckled. "I'm as open as a backyard. Have to be, around here."

The sheriff gave him a glare. Eric looked away quickly. The sheriff walked a wide arc to the left side of the cabin. Behind it was an open area. Unusually open. More open than a person with a chainsaw would make in an old growth forest. "Squashed trees." She clicked on her walkie. "This is the right place, Eric. Good job."

Then there was a crash and Eric yelled. "Fuck me!"

The sheriff had her revolver out as she ran back on the wide arc, just in time to see a clear ball of something squash the department's *all-situations vehicle* while Eric dove away from it.

The sheriff turned to find a gaping hole in the front of the cabin. There stood a dirty little man in his underwear, pointing a box at her. The sheriff shot twice, low, and high. The man went down as a massive clear ball of something jumped in the air toward her. She, too, dived to the side as the clear ball crashed down on the trees beside her cruiser.

Eric ran up to the cabin and grabbed the box from the wounded man's hands. "Great shot, Iceberg! You got the box. And the perp." Eric laughed and then made a face. He didn't mean to call the sheriff by one of her nicknames. "Sorry, Sheriff Willisburg. I was just excited. Meant no disrespect."

The sheriff waved him off. "This guy's Randall Slater, I guess?" The dirty little guy held his bleeding leg but was also unconscious.

"Yeah." Eric burped. "Arrested him myself a few years back. Didn't bathe then either." Eric held his nose.

"Wrap him in some blankets and put him in the cruiser. I want to look around this shithole a bit before we leave." The sheriff stepped over some debris. "Oh, and call in for a team to come out here to do a more thorough search. Oh, and get an ETM out here for him."

"Good. They hosed him down." The sheriff stood by Slater's bedside in the town clinic. "He asked for a lawyer?"

Eric shook his head. "Just a drink, any type of scotch." Eric chuckled. "A drunk by any other name still smells."

The sheriff tipped her head down to look at him. "Not as much as before. Thankfully. He's conscious then?"

Eric shrugged.

The sheriff smacked Slater on his hairy cheek. "Wakey, wakey! Time to start lying."

Slater opened one eye.

"You weren't unconscious. Lied without saying a word. Great accomplishment." The sheriff held out a bag of twenty-dollar bills. "You a bill collector?"

Eric laughed.

Slater said, "What?"

"And this?" The sheriff held out the box she had shot. The bullet hole was dead center.

"Oh, you broke it." Slater stared at it sadly.

"Don't tell me you found this in the woods," she said.

"I did." Slater frowned.

"She told you not to say that. You deaf?" Eric slammed his hand on the side of the bed.

It made the sheriff chuckle as Slater looked confused. "Yeah, think of a better lie. Oh, and there is the murder of Jesse Pimbolt."

"No, Jesse kilt hisself." Slater attempted to sit up but failed. "He didn't know how it worked. The box. He was showing me what he got." Slater shook his head. "Pushed the button with the box turned toward hisself." Slater looked sick. "Then squash! I grabbed the box and runned off." Slater looked at the sheriff. "Ya believe me, right?"

"He's no alien though, sheriff." Eric chuckled.

"What?" Slater looked at the Sheriff. "I's born American."

The sheriff shook her head. "Just one more thing. Where did Pimbolt get the box? And no *finding it in the woods* mega-vulture shit."

"Stole it." Slater stated.

"There ya go." The sheriff handed the box to Eric. "From where?"

"That defense contractor over there on the mountain," Slater said. "So, I'm free cause of the information I just gived?"

"No, there is a squashed ATM you will be charged with, but I'll talk to the judge. Maybe get it reduced from robbery to mechanical assault." The sheriff stood up.

"What about my squashed *all-situations vehicle*?" Eric said.

"Department's actually, but the judge will judge that too." The sheriff took the box from Eric and left.

"Can I get a drink now?" Slater asked weakly.

"Ah? No!" Eric answered.

*GLS Corporation* looked big and empty. It appeared more a compound than a business complex. High chain-link fences with razor wire surrounded it. The parking lot was middle sized but had few vehicles in it. Except for a few security guards, the place seemed deserted. The sheriff sat in the large lobby with Deputy Eric.

"Empty," Eric declared. "Never liked big empty places."

"You have agoraphobia?" The sheriff twirled her hat on her left hand.

"No." Eric looked confused. "Just don't like large open spaces." He continued to pace. "Should have called first."

"I thought you had." She stopped twirling.

"Meant to, but I, ah, needed to get another vehicle. I loved my old *all-situations vehicle*. Hard to break in a new one." He paced faster.

"They are all the same." The sheriff stood up. "Still, you were supposed to call here and ask about any break-ins."

Eric stopped pacing. "Has to be an inside job. Look at the security here."

Right then a Mercedes pulled up at the front door and a man in an expensive business suit got out and walked into the lobby. "Sheriff Willisburg?" The man held his hand out.

She shook his hand. "Yes."

"You should have called ahead, and we would not have made you wait. We apologize." The man smiled a professional smile. "I am GSL Head Consul, Helmut Zane."

"No, we are sorry. Well, the deputy here is sorrier." The sheriff looked over at Eric. Eric looked down at the expensive floor. "But no problem. Thank you for seeing us on short notice."

"Come into the conference room over here." Mr. Zane motioned toward a far door. He waited until the sheriff and the deputy walked toward it, and then he followed.

The conference room appeared to be only slightly smaller than the lobby. You could hold a real conference in it. Deputy Eric shivered as he sat at the large table. The sheriff just rolled her eyes at him. There was coffee, tea, orange juice and bottled water on the table before them.

"We could get some food sent up, if you like?" Mr. Zane sat down beside them.

"No, thank you. Very unnecessary. But thank you," the sheriff said as Eric poured himself a big glass of orange juice. "We came to ask about something we found in the woods." The sheriff placed the box on the dark walnut table. The pale sides of the box appeared anemic in contrast to the richness of the walnut.

Mr. Zane glanced at the box but said nothing.

The sheriff tipped her head toward the box and raised her eyebrows. Eric poured another glass of orange juice.

Mr. Zane pulled out his mobile phone and texted someone.

"A comment?" the sheriff asked.

"Not yet," Mr. Zane answered.

"Not yet?" The Sheriff hadn't expected this answer.

"One moment please." He said. "I have asked the head of the company to join us."

"Okay, if you want." The sheriff shook her head at Eric for pouring his third glass of orange juice.

Another door in the back of the room slid open silently. In walked three very short figures in white lab coats, all with very long noses and pointed ears.

"Aliens!" Eric muttered and almost dropped his third glass of OJ.

The sheriff remained quiet but was happy not to have had anything in her hands. Mr. Zane smiled professionally.

"Sheriff Willisburg, this is Dr. Handle Friget, GSL's CEO and President." Mr. Zane indicated as the three individuals sat down.

"Please call me Han, Sheriff Willisburg." His face was covered with short tan fur. It was darker around his eyes, like a mask. When he smiled, his pronounced canine teeth showed. He waved his padded palmed hand at the two individuals beside him. "This is GSL's head of R and D, Pika Bushtail, ME, PhD. She's a great engineer despite her small size. And Dr. CL 7893. He's a traditionalist, so don't comment on his name." Han and Pika laughed a chattering laugh. CL 7893 obviously was not amused.

"Aliens?" Eric rudely muttered again. The sheriff shushed him. It generated a chattering laugh from all three of them now.

"They are Gnomes, not aliens," Mr. Zane stated after the laughter died down.

"Our stealth strategy has been too successful, it appears, CL." Han moved his furry snout up and down.

"Better this way." Dr. CL 7893 growled.

"Gnomes, but that's just a myth." Eric muttered. "That was just a show."

"A Gnome show?" The sheriff asked. All three resident Gnomes gave the affirmative gesture with their furry heads.

"A show. I saw it as a kid." Eric was confused. "Puppets. Midgets in raccoon costumes. A musical show."

"A show about Gnomes?" The sheriff was confused too. "I'm not from Seattle. Ah, sorry for this confusion."

"No, no. We have been flying under the radar for the last decade just because of this reaction." Han smiled his toothy smile.

"Intelligent resuscitated prehistoric raccoons make some humans uncomfortable." Dr. Bushtail's voice was very pleasant.

"The reason the Institute called us Gnomes," Han grumbled.

"I preferred Troll." Dr. CL 7893 hissed.

"That wouldn't have helped, CL," Dr. Bushtail chattered.

Han waved at the wall. "GSL, Gnome Land Security Corporation. Gnomes have to have a sense of humor."

"Not a very good one," Dr. CL 7893 muttered.

"So, you brought us something you found in the woods?" Han pointed at the box.

"Who shot it?" Dr. CL 7893 barked.

"Sheriff did. Great shooting too." Eric tried to help.

"Oh, clotted butt fur!" Dr. CL 7893 barked again.

"CL! Excuse me! Lady here!" Dr. Bushtail growled.

"Sorry, but I had to. Didn't want to get squashed." The sheriff felt unbalanced by this weird mega-vulture shit. "What is it?"

"We don't actually know." Han sighed.

"What did it do?" Dr. Bushtail asked so nicely that all the sheriff could do was answer truthfully.

"It projects a ball of energy, I guess. Wouldn't you say Eric?" Eric blinked in response. "This ball of energy is so powerful it can squash a car or a person."

Eric pushed his unpadded palms together. "Flattened, just like that."

"You don't know what it can do, and you created it?" The sheriff pointed at the box.

"We didn't create it." Han shook his furry head back and forth, but his ears remained directed toward the sheriff.

"Sounds like we would want to," barked Dr. CL 7893.

"You found it in the woods?" the sheriff said weakly.

Dr. Bushtail nodded.

Mr. Zane then shook his non-furry head.

Han looked at Dr. CL 7893 and nodded. Dr. CL 7893 nodded back. Han nodded to Mr. Zane. Mr. Zane shook his head again, but Han countered with a nod and a furry head tilt toward the sheriff.

"Nondisclosure agreements then?" Mr. Zane finally uttered.

Han shook his head. "If we can't trust the sheriff, who can we trust?"

"No one," Mr. Zane muttered. "Is best."

Han waved off the comment and waved at Dr. Bushtail to proceed.

"Found it in our dig in the back. It is why the facility is here."
Dr. Bushtail wrinkled her rostrum cutely. "We first found pieces of
a craft. Dr. Pika Lushlash actually discovered it while on a hike with
a few other gnomes. For us, the more remote the better. They found
a crash-site. We started to dig."

"Alien craft!" Eric blurted.

"Only conclusion to make," Dr. CL 7893 blurted back.

"So, alien that it is very difficult to get a handle on. Ah, pardon
the pun." Han smiled.

"Caution! Extreme caution, too extreme made things, makes
things precede slowly. So much other stuff!" Dr. CL 7893 growled.
"Hadn't gotten to the box yet."

"Not cautious enough to prevent it from being stolen." The
sheriff wanted to regain control of the very weird situation. *I really
hate weird,* she kept thinking.

"Yes! Apparently." Han glanced over to Mr. Zane. He gave no
response, verbal or nonverbal.

"*X-Files* meets *The Island of Dr. Moreau*," Eric muttered. "Far
fuckin' out!"

"Deputy!" the sheriff snapped. Gnome chatter and laughter
followed.

"Good one, deputy," Dr. Bushtail commented.

"Yeah, I like it!" Dr. CL 7893 smiled broadly and scarily. It was
an all-sharp toothed smile.

"Despite all of this goodwill and humor, the box is *GSL's*
property." Mr. Zane always remained professional.

"Want it back to study." Dr. CL 7893 tapped his claws on the
walnut table. "Pictures of what it did would be good, too."

"I am certain the sheriff understands our perspective," Dr.
Bushtail almost whispered.

The sheriff rubbed her nose with her unpadded palm. "Weird
makes my nose itch. Sorry."

"Mine, too." Dr. Bushtail grinned. "It's why I'm in research."

The sheriff looked around the table. All eyes, no matter what
the species, were looking back at her. She was finally in control of
the situation. Everyone had delegated the decision on the weird to
the sheriff's authority.

"I could start court proceedings," Mr. Zane interrupted, but
everyone glared at him.

"No. No need. We can work this out." The sheriff shook her head. "Just part of my job. Working the weird. Pearly will love this."

"Pearly? Is that your significant other?" Dr. Bushtail waved her bushy tail in the air along with a sharp-toothed grin.

"Yes, she is." The sheriff chuckled. "So, significant, yes. She is also my lawyer."

# About the Author

Michael W. Clark has a PhD. in molecular biology from U.C.L.A. He has been a research scientist as well as an entrepreneur. Along with these professional endeavors, he has been writing fiction and poetry since he was a teenager. He is the creator, editor, and contributor for the fiction and non-fiction website, www.ahickshope.wordpress.com. He presently lives in Santa Monica, CA.

# The Calypso Deadlock
by
Fulvio Gatti

# The Calypso Deadlock

**PR** specialist Vittorio Bartoli believed the worldwide opening of the Ausonia Lifestyle&Food in Downtown Manhattan would be the peak of his career. He had no idea he would only remember the shiny dining rooms, the dozens of well-trained personnel, the wealthy patrons complimenting the tasty, unique dishes from his country as part of *that last job before the Alien thing.*

It was the middle of the night in his North Bergen apartment, at the end of a frantic day of meetings. He kept idly going through a few debriefing details. Meanwhile, in a conference call from Torino, his associate Marta was reading aloud and sometimes commenting on some budget issues.

Vittorio trusted Marta's ability with the money part, so he simply listened to her voice, glancing at the screen from time to time, every time looking away, embarrassed by how strongly he still was attracted to her. There had been a time, before, they had been so close that people thought they were a couple. But life, work, and Vittorio's selfishness had gotten in the way. The pragmatic attitude they were proud of, being from the Piemonte region, had eventually set things straight between them; they were excellent at working together, and nothing else.

Vittorio was trying to decide whether to keep a picture of him with an Italian CEO who'd recently passed away—he doubted anyone would remember the guy in a few years—when he realized Marta wasn't talking anymore. He raised his eyes to the screen only to see her frowning at a phone call, almost pushing the phone into her ear. Her face turned pale, and she intently focused on the conversation, muttering monosyllables. Vittorio couldn't tell if she was more puzzled or worried.

Marta ended the conversation, and she met his glance, sighing.

"Was it…Satan that wants to hire us for the upcoming Apocalypse?" Vittorio asked, trying to fill the void with a joke that sounded more unsettling than expected.

Marta barely grinned. "Not exactly…but also, not too far off," she replied.

"What kind of job is *not too far* from Armageddon itself?" Vittorio insisted.

Marta's face turned serious like she hadn't even heard his last words. "They are coming to get you," she announced in a plain voice. "The American Government—US Army or something."

"What?" Vittorio burst out. "Am I under arrest?"

"Not that you don't deserve it, with all those barely-adult women you've been flirting with lately," Marta replied.

At any other time, Vittorio would have enjoyed the hint of jealousy coming across with her words. Instead, he simply started breathing again; it wasn't too bad, or she wouldn't be using irony.

"They have a job for you." Her expression darkened. "Only, they make the rules."

Less than half an hour later two tall men in black clothing knocked at his door. They showed their badges and introduced themselves as Thompson and Smythe, agents of *The Department. Unspecified.* Kind but firm, they asked Vittorio to collect his belongings for a week-long trip, let him prepare the luggage, and then led him out of the building without wasting a single breath.

What followed was a silent journey in the back seat of a limo, Smythe sitting by his side and ignoring any attempt at conversation. Vittorio ended up texting a few messages to a worried Marta. When she eventually told him how much the job paid, his mood suddenly brightened.

The limo reached a private airport and Vittorio and his luggage were loaded onto a small aircraft, its engines already running. *So, this is serious,* he thought. Not that his usual customers weren't used to private planes; still, very few of them considered it essential to have the PR guy fly that way. It was why he had ended up facing the extra expense of a New Jersey apartment. Not to mention how important it was to put an ocean between him and his associate as things had started getting complicated.

The flight was short. Vittorio wasn't good enough in geography to guess their destination by the time spent in the air. Washington was as good a guess as another. A second limo, this time with tinted windows, brought them to the rear parking lot of an anonymous public building. The agents led Vittorio to an elevator that carried them ten floors underground: a proper bunker to handle ultra-secret stuff.

Their final destination was an empty office with a generic world map on the wall. Vittorio took his seat in front of the only desk and was almost immediately left alone by the agents. He checked his phone, noticing that there was no signal. A possible consequence for being underground or another secrecy measure.

Out of a tiny door came a short, slim man, with big glasses and a shadow of a white mustache covering his thin mouth. His dressing style was so inconspicuous that Vittorio needed a further look to recognize it was indeed a military uniform.

"Mr. Bartoli, I'm General Wight. Thank you for accepting our invitation." The military man spoke in a direct but flat voice. "Before we begin, I need you to sign an NDA."

The general handed him a folder of documents. Vittorio grabbed it and skimmed through the pages.

"We'd also appreciate…quick execution, Mr. Bartoli," the general stated.

Vittorio gave the stranger a skeptical look. "Everything I learn here, I must keep it to myself forever, right?" he suggested.

"Exactly."

Vittorio grunted softly, signed, and pushed the folder back.

"Of course, you know about the supposed storming of Area 51 last month, Mr. Bartoli?" the general asked.

Vittorio grinned. "Bunch of idiots spending too much time on Facebook?"

"So, I suppose you are familiar with the Roswell accident as well?" the general continued.

Vittorio held his breath. "P-please?" he managed to reply.

"In 1947, in New Mexico, an Unidentified Flying Object…" the general begun.

Vittorio giggled. "I know about it. The aliens, the autopsy…everything!" he said in an amused voice. "As a kid I was fond of the story…"

"Good," General Wight replied without losing his aplomb.

Vittorio blinked. "Wait. Is that what the job is about?"

"Correct," General Wight replied again.

Vittorio took a deep breath. "All right, since *this*"—he hinted at the bare underground office—"cannot be a joke, I guess it's for real. So, what's my job?"

General Wight seemed to appreciate his bluntness. "You will have access to all our documents about UFOs and close encounters with extra-terrestrial life on this planet and its close proximity. I should add that it's the biggest archive mankind has ever had on the topic. We need you to decide what to leak next, when, and how."

Vittorio grimaced. "Leak?"

The shadow of a grin appeared on the general's face. "We are very good at handling information, Mr. Bartoli. So much that we even decide when to let something out through unofficial channels."

Vittorio smirked back. "Quite impressive indeed."

"We are living in strange times, Mr. Bartoli," General Wight continued. "Thanks to the Internet, a group of strangers from around the world can not only exchange information about government secrets, they may even, with little effort, decide they'll enter Area 51 on a certain date and time. And eventually do that."

Vittorio remembered forgetting about the whole Internet stunt after making fun of it with some friends. "Oh, yeah… How did it end? They found the aliens?" Vittorio asked.

"They found nothing relevant," the general replied, pursing his lips in displeasure.

"Too bad," Vittorio commented without thinking. He then frowned. "It's because you knew about the visit and moved the aliens and all the stuff away?" His words still felt a bit odd. The very idea of Area 51 aliens being real was way too silly.

General Wight stared at Vittorio. "Yes…and no. They only proved that the good old ways are outdated. We need a new way, and we need it from you."

Something in General Wight's eyes told Vittorio their conversation was over. He had no idea about what to do next, but he could still pretend enthusiasm.

"*Va bene.* How do I begin?"

Vittorio had a huge archive to explore and a room where he could study and rest. Through a side closet he had access to fresh food and clean clothes, not to mention a comfortable bathroom with a bathtub. No *bidet*, but nobody is perfect. As long as he stayed in the archive or his room, nobody would bother him. It was the perfect setting for intense research.

There was a catalog of the archive content. It took a few hours, but eventually Vittorio was able to understand it and set up a research plan. The amount of information to go through was stunning. He was both excited and overwhelmed at the same time. He found a dossier about the Nazca Lines, then another about the Bermuda Triangle. When he finally put his hands on the complete transcription of Jesse Marcel's memoirs, he knew where to start.

The author was the military man who had found the debris from the flying saucer in Roswell in 1947. His superior officers had later stated that it was only a balloon, so the story had disappeared from the press. But Marcel himself had brought it back in 1978: it was the beginning of the legend as the general public knew it.

Vittorio kept reading until he fell asleep at the desk. An automatic clock woke him up at 6 a.m., his back aching and his head dizzy. He took a shower, then decided to set up a routine. He'd choose a path, explore it in a rational way, then stop for lunch. On the second half of the day, he would decide whether to pursue the path or to try something new.

The first three days were pure exploration. Frantic and hungry for knowledge, Vittorio kept jumping between topics. Sometimes his juvenile hypotheses were confirmed, other times they were totally subverted. The most shocking discovery was that the Moon Landing was indeed a fake—during the trip to the satellite, the rocket had been escorted by UFOs.

On the sixth day, General Wight came for a brief visit to check his progress. Vittorio felt a subtle pressure: they expected results and expected them soon. The first proper discovery was how UFO sightings had dramatically declined in the 21st century. Vittorio tried to find a reason for that but only stumbled over more mysteries.

As time passed, Vittorio grew less and less happy about his job. He found himself going over the same stories again and again, unable to make anything of them. What surprised him the most was that the truth in the secret documents was not too far from urban legends told by sensational books and magazines. The general was right: the apparent leaks about UFOs were nothing but disguised press releases that had found their place in the public's collective imagination.

Aliens had visited humanity for thousands of years. They came in various kinds and races, from different planets and galaxies. By the beginning of the 20th century, one specific race, the Greys, had begun visiting Earth more frequently. They traveled our skies in their flying saucers and sometimes, accidentally, they fell on the ground. After some UFO crashes in North America, alien corpses and a few survivors had been found. One alien had been captured and held hostage in Area 51. All attempts at communication had failed and the extra-terrestrial visitor had eventually died.

All the documents confirmed that. The story was solid. And, simply, dead. It was a Calypso Deadlock. Recognizing the original expression he had created for one of his marketing books didn't make Vittorio happier. A good story killed by its very potential, stuck in its own storytelling. Even the greatest of the storytellers, Ulysses, had eventually been trapped in his own narrative, while he was being held prisoner by the nymph Calypso in *The Odyssey*.

Vittorio spent his twelfth day in the bunker in his bed trying to sleep. He had blurred dreams about balloons mistaken for flying saucers and dwarflike corpses passed off as alien bodies.

In the morning of the thirteenth day, General Wight came to visit him.

"I guess reading is not enough anymore, Mr. Bartoli," he stated, ignoring Vittorio's complaints. "It's time for you to finally see."

Vittorio had a shower and then breakfast. When he felt ready, he joined General Wight and agents Thompson and Smythe. Seeing his former escort made him smile. But, remembering the time before the bunker had him longing to get out. He wanted to breathe fresh air again. He wanted to see Marta. The memory made his chest ache.

Smythe and Thompson pushed him along an apparently infinite hallway. Vittorio's steps were heavy. He saw no reason to go with them. Only an intense look from General Wight was able to shake him.

"You'll see. And then you'll understand," he stated.

At the end of the walk, they found themselves in front of a narrow door. The general typed a code on a small keyboard and the door opened. Vittorio could only see a dim light inside. They entered, leaving the agents outside.

It took a while for Vittorio's eyes to recognize anything in the room. It was similar to his own, with essential pieces of furniture and no decoration, except for a platform in the middle. Looking closer he saw something on the platform.

Vittorio blinked, not believing his very eyes.

"Can you see, now?" the general said, a hint of expectation in his voice.

Vittorio stared at the humanoid figure—head too large, arms and legs too thin and short. It was a Grey Alien: familiar and repelling at the same time. Just as Vittorio was getting used to the unexpected presence, the alien opened his eyes wide. They were as black as darkness itself. Vittorio couldn't help but step back.

"He is...alive?" he asked. His voice echoed in the room.

"Correct," the general whispered.

The alien slowly turned his head, his huge black eyes on Vittorio. He felt all the weight of the glare, and a little shiver ran through his spine. Vittorio started breathing fast, his brain trying to collect the pieces. Part of him wished he had never accepted the job. He wanted to go back to his usual life, struggling to find a good gig even if it meant navigating through politics, competitors, and everyday nuisances. But the rest of him knew how good it was in this other—the one he had always dreamed of. The one that was finally displaying itself in front of his eyes.

"Can I...get closer?" Vittorio asked, already moving toward the platform and the alien. He got no answer from the general and barely felt his presence by his side.

"Can we...communicate?" Vittorio spoke again. This time, addressing the alien.

The Grey moved its head in what might pass for a nod. Many questions exploded in Vittorio's head. Was it a common gesture among humanoid creatures? Or was it maybe something the visitor had learned by dwelling on Earth? And in any case, was it the same creature saved from the Roswell accident? The paper said it was dead.

Vittorio's heart missed a beat as he saw the alien *changing*, not just moving. The opening that might have been its mouth was widening, finding its way through the surface of the big head. The semicircular hole was getting larger and larger. Inside it, Vittorio was suddenly able to recognize one...no, two, three, four...a whole line of pointy, shiny fangs. The smooth grey skin wasn't there anymore, instead covered by thick brown fur, while pointy, furred ears, like those of a wolf, or a lion, or a bear appeared near the back.

A feral, hideous creature rose from the platform on its four clawed legs. It jumped toward Vittorio before he could react. The fangs and the claws shone in the dim light while Vittorio felt, deep inside, that he knew what to do next. If only he could survive the beast.

"Marta!" Vittorio shrieked, or at least he tried to.

His mouth made a weak, muffled sound. It took a few seconds for his hazed eyes to recognize the human figure in front of him. It was General Wight. The military man stood beside his bed. Vittorio was in his room, the bunker room, with an IV in his arm.

"You'll see your associate soon, Mr. Bartoli," the general explained. "But you need to recover first. And then, of course, finish your job."

Vittorio felt that the nightmare wasn't over yet. He tried to focus on the money he'd receive, but he found himself struggling against the impossible memory of a fanged creature attacking him.

"What…what happened?" he asked.

"You had quite a shock, Mr. Bartoli. You've been unconscious for three days," the general replied.

Vittorio took a long breath, checking along his body to see if there was anything wrong.

"What did you see in the room?" the general asked, squinting at him.

Vittorio let out a cough and stared back. "What did *you* see, general?"

The military man looked away, at though recalling an old memory. "Some kind of devil with Middle Eastern features," he said, without meeting his eyes. "I guess having found my personal Hell in Iraq left some waste in my own, deepest fears…"

Vittorio felt like the military man had loosened up.

"They appear…different…to everyone?" Vittorio asked.

"It's more complicated than that," the general replied. He had reverted back to his usual coldness. "They are…changing. We used to be able to control them, restrain them into a big, consistent, even if absurd, single story. That was before. Now they are breaking free. People are disappearing, there are terrorist attacks as well as meaningless acts of violence all over the planet. It's them, stronger than ever."

The general gave him an intense look. "This is why your job is urgent."

Vittorio held his breath. "But why me? What about Stephen King or some other imaginative writer?"

"We can't trust an artist. Their creations could go wild and become dangerous. We need a professional to fix a story," General Wight said. "You can fix a broken story, can't you?"

Vittorio recognized the title of his bestselling book from 2010. The Calypso Deadlock was one of the seven case histories he had found fancy names for. So ironic that something written out of pure passion had made him work for Olmo Marinetti, the founder of Ausonia Lifestyle&Food, first, and would eventually lead to all this.

Vittorio did his best to get back to work as soon as possible. Thanks to discipline, he was able to immerse himself in full-time research. He knew the original urban legend, he knew how it had turned into a new, contemporary mythology. Now, decades later, the same stories weren't captivating anymore. Harsh reality, like wars and terrorism, was far more threatening for 21st century citizens.

Vittorio began studying the legends about the Reptilians. Their expected presence on Earth seemed to be more recent and had nothing to do with the Roswell accident. In their most common version, Reptilians were a shape-shifting race secretly ruling Earth against the will of poor little humans. YouTube videos tried to demonstrate how presidents and kings from all over the world were in fact wicked aliens in disguise.

Vittorio had always had little interest in this theory because it lacked any logic and was extremely self-indulgent for the believer: I'm poor and a failure because some bad alien secretly controls my life. Also, he suspected the development of these specific urban legends had been deeply influenced by movies like *They Live* and tv shows like *V*. No, it was not the kind of story for him now.

Vittorio spent a full day taking notes on a third branch of the UFO mythology, the one referring to angelic beings visiting Earth to save humanity. In some versions, those good and beautiful aliens were the bosses of the Greys. Since people still believed in the Greys enough to try and visit Area 51, it was a starting point.

What if the best story to restrain the alien presence on Earth was the Good Angels? Urban legends were close to religion in the way they needed believers to work properly. Maybe the Catholics and Christians all over the planet would help this version find its place in the collective imagination...

Vittorio almost yelled at General Wight as the military man paid him a visit. Vittorio babbled about angels and demons, good will and last hope, receiving a perplexed gaze in reply. Getting control of himself, Vittorio was eventually able to ask the general to leave him alone.

But as the military man left the room, Vittorio kicked the wall in anger. He let himself fall over the bed and let himself sink onto the mattress, without a single ounce of energy left in his body. His mind was empty, and the Good Angels story was crap. It would never stick. A part of him had dreamed about it, the child inside that a long time ago wanted to become a sci-fi writer.

The visit from the general had brought the adult Vittorio back to himself. He was a PR guy, not a writer. He had created stories for years for the sole purpose of selling goods, not to tell the truth, but to take advantage of the feelings of inadequacy, fear of loneliness and death, and have people spend their money on things they didn't really need. Capitalism had driven most of mankind's lives for decades, thanks to selfishness and hatred. Nothing *good* would ever be taken for granted by anyone. Everyone fed off conflict, rivalries, hunger, and hate...

*Hate.*

The four-letter word bounced around in Vittorio's skull. There was a distant memory trying to surface from the thousands of pages he had been reading. His instinct said *Roswell.* Could it be possible that the solution was there, back at the beginning?

Vittorio rushed into the archive. He collected all the folders connected to the UFO crash in New Mexico. He knew which ones were useful and which ones were not because some memories from the witnesses simply didn't fit with the overall story. *And that's the point.*

Folders in hand, Vittorio rushed to his desk, turned on the laptop and started writing. He had to stop before he collapsed on the keyboard. He felt relieved, since he knew this was finally the right path. But he had to write it down, and to do it immediately! He ate some chocolate while he made a cup of coffee. It was not Italian coffee, but it would keep him awake.

Vittorio wrote like crazy through the night. The digital clock marked *6:16* when he was finally able to put the last line to his report. Five thousand words and it sounded right. He ripped the top sheet from his notebook and wrote a note for General Wight: *Your story is ready, wake me up when you see this message.* He put it on the ground, in front of his door, and went to sleep.

If he expected enthusiasm from a military man, he was disappointed. The morning after, when Vittorio told him the work was done, the general simply nodded and took away the laptop. A couple of days passed without Vittorio hearing anything from anyone. He relaxed, ate, slept, and tried not to think about how much he needed a walk in the park, preferably with Marta. On the third day he began to suspect they were going to leave him there, but then Thompson and Smythe showed up, silent and efficient as usual.

In the limo heading back to the airplane, Vittorio was able to text Marta. She replied that the payment was already in his bank account. *Off to a good start.*

Marta was at the airport waiting for him. She wore a short-sleeved shirt with a floral pattern the same shade of cyan as her eyes. A blue skirt covered a small portion of her long legs, and she even wore high-heels, so she stood as tall as him. Vittorio struggled against the urge to take her in his arms and kiss her. Still, something in her eyes told him that he was not the only one yearning for some intimacy.

She drove him home, but along the way they agreed to meet later for dinner. Time moved on quickly as Vittorio showered and then shaved his beard. He chose from his wardrobe an indigo suit, his favorite. He took his old Citroen—soon to be replaced by a brand-new car—and reached Marta's house ten minutes early. She was by the entrance, waiting for him.

He stepped out of the car to open the door for her. She smiled at him and gracefully hopped inside. As Vittorio got back into his seat, he turned to her and saw those blue eyes shining with joy. He leaned toward her and touched her lips with his. They kissed and it was like the world around them had suddenly faded away.

After a delicious appetizer and a glass of sparkling wine, movement on the giant television in the middle of the dining room caught their attention. Marta had to turn to watch it. The news reported a series of UFO sightings all over the world.

Marta squinted at Vittorio. "It has to do with you, right?"

Vittorio gave her a proud glance. "I just did my job." He paused. "A very good result, for a very well-paid gig…" He chuckled.

"I know it's like asking a magician to reveal his tricks but…aren't UFOs a bit of a vintage thing?" she asked. "I hadn't heard of them since, well, the eighties…"

Vittorio shrugged. "They were. Just trust me, here, when I say that we have been in extreme danger. Remember the Armageddon joke? That's close."

Marta burst out in an adorable laugh. "You're mocking me, aren't you?"

Vittorio couldn't help laughing back, while fighting against some unsettling imagery from the bunker and its unexpected resident. He shook the memories away. The job was done, and in a brilliant way. There was nothing left to fear.

"Remember my book about fixing stories? Let's say I did it in the right way. A good story for the future; the story that mankind wants to hear."

Marta was getting restless. "How many times do I have to ask you, before you'll finally tell me?"

Vittorio tried to ignore what he saw on the TV screen. A burning skyscraper in New York. A fallen bridge in Munich. A fire squad digging in the ruins of a French building. *This has nothing to do with me*, he said to himself.

"Please…" Marta said.

Vittorio blinked. The stunning blue eyes of his partner gave him the energy to speak. "It was a misinterpretation of all of the Roswell memories that gave me the idea. There was not a single UFO crash in New Mexico in 1947—there were two."

"I remember reading something," Marta replied. "The other one was in Corona, right?"

"Correct," Vittorio said. He couldn't help thinking about General Wight.

Marta pursed her lips. "Why would two UFO crashes instead of one mean something different?"

"Two, and even more. I discovered no less than ten accidents in three years. Either those poor Grey aliens had terrible driving skills or…"

"They shot them down!" Marta exclaimed, brightened. "Was it…a war?"

"I'd rather call it…an alien invasion, proudly stopped by our great Western Army!" Vittorio announced.

On the screen, an old man was being interviewed. In the noise, they distinctly heard the word "invaders."

"It was the forties, then the fifties and the sixties," Vittorio continued. "People needed hope. They wanted to imagine visitors from space, peaceful ones. But that time is gone. The Roswell accident is a story from the past. What's the only thing that unifies people all over the world, nowadays?"

Marta smirked. "I have an idea…"

"Hate, my dear. Old, rusty, powerful hate," Vittorio stated. "People today don't want dreams anymore. They only yearn for someone to hate."

Vittorio raised his glass of wine, staring into Marta's eyes. His arm ached underneath his shirt. Vittorio pulled the sleeve up to see a deep, partially recovered cut. He could picture the claws of the furry alien in front of him. While Marta asked about the injury, worried, Vittorio finally understood. It wasn't a good story anymore. It was real war.

Tears blurred Vittorio Bartoli's sight as he gave one last look at the love of his life. *Pardon me, if you ever could.*

Then the ceiling blew up and the whole building collapsed.

# About the Author

Fulvio Gatti is an Italian speculative fiction writer and has been writing and publishing in his native tongue for 25 years. He has been writing in English for the global market since 2018. His stories can be found in pro magazines, like Galaxy's Edge, magazines and anthologies published in US, UK, Canada, Northern Europe and Australia.

He's been a student of Kevin J. Anderson and Rebecca Moesta's Superstars Writing Seminars and part of Dave Wolverton's Apex Writing Group. He's also been a panelist at Worldcon/Discon III, among other international events. Since 2022, he's been a SFWA associate member. He lives with his wife and daughter on the vineyard-rich hills of Northwestern Italy, where he works as a local reporter and event organizer.

# Crop Circles and Werewolves
by
John M. Campbell

# Crop Circles and Werewolves

**A** rumble of thunder on a clear night alerted Garry to the fireball plummeting overhead. The object streaking through the sky was not a meteor. The tint of its ultraviolet emissions identified it as a Chupian vehicle, and he traced its trajectory to the mountain foothills a few kilometers away. A wave of resignation passed through his body.

If this Chupe was anything like its predecessors, the cattle mutilations would begin soon. The Chupes came to Earth for one reason only: the fresh, prime beef. Garry had one opportunity to warn them off. He would construct a crop circle. And he'd best do it before morning.

As he did each time before venturing outside, he pulled on his boots to hide his three-toed feet and pulled on his gloves to hide his eight-fingered hands. The flannel shirt and denim jeans covered the dense layer of fur on his body. The Stetson went on last. A mini-holo unit nestled inside the crown of his hat provided the face and voice he needed to pass as human.

He left the comfortably chilly confines of his tiny cabin and walked past his vegetable garden to the barn. He swung open the wide doors. Although the barn appeared empty, his saucer was stashed inside, protected by its own holographic camouflage. With the remote he'd installed on his human-made smartwatch, Garry opened the hatch on the vehicle. An oval hole appeared in the hologram to reveal the pilot's seat inside. He gathered together his crop circle tools, climbed in, and shut the hatch.

Starting up the saucer, he felt the familiar floating sensation as power from the fusion reactor flowed into the antigrav engines and lifted the saucer off the ground. He rotated the ship until its forward cameras faced the open doors of the barn. Then he inched ahead to emerge into the darkness.

When in flight, Garry's saucer did not produce enough extra power to maintain the holographic cloaking field. So, crop circles were best crafted in darkness when casual observers would have difficulty seeing his vehicle. Tonight, the moon had already set, perfect conditions for circle-making.

Garry flew the short hop to the plot of long prairie grass he cultivated for just such a purpose. Hovering over the center of the plot, he gently lowered the saucer until it came to rest on the ground. He rotated the ship three times to imprint a magnetic circle into the soil and create the signature spiral pattern in the grass.

Now for his favorite part. Grabbing his board, stakes, and ropes, he stepped from the ship. He placed his back against the edge of the saucer and sidestepped around until he faced the North Star. Attached to one end of the long rope he carried was a stake that he pushed into the ground. He tromped out a straight line through the grass toward the north star. When he reached the ten-meter mark on the rope, he inserted another stake. Attached to the end of his board was another rope that he looped around this second stake. Using this stake as a hub, he stretched the rope to its length. With his arms pressing on the board, he flattened the grass into a doughnut shape. Then he placed one end of the board against the stake and rotated the board around it to flatten the remaining grass around the center. The result was a circle four meters in diameter.

Removing the stake, he tromped a straight line outward toward the North Star for another five meters. He crafted a quick two-meter circle. Returning to the saucer, he repeated the procedure every sixty degrees around the edge—but only four more times. He left the last 120-degree sector untouched. Crop circle enthusiasts always loved a bit of mystery.

Reentering his ship, Garry took to the sky to view his creation. By starlight, the whimsical pattern he created in the grass was barely visible. Of more importance was the magnetic signature he left in the soil. The circular warning sign shined brightly on his scope. Its meaning would be unmistakable when the Chupe detected it. It meant, "Clear out. This territory is occupied."

A few days later, the buzz of a single-engine aircraft passed overhead. A change in pitch and volume told Garry it had altered its course. He went outside. The plane had turned back to take another look at the crop circle. That night, a picture of it appeared on the internet.

The next day, Garry heard the crunch of gravel on the road that ended at his cabin. A news van rolled up. Garry walked out to greet the young reporter and his cameraman.

"I'm Clark Canton from the *Cripple Creek Courier*."

Garry responded with a slow tip of his Stetson.

"I understand there's a crop circle nearby?" Clark Canton asked.

"Yup." Garry had streamed old westerns to train his holo voice to sound like a cowboy.

"Can I see it?"

"I reckon."

The reporter waited to hear more. Garry just stared at him.

"Can you tell me where I might find it?"

"Yonder," Garry said and lifted a gloved finger to point.

"Yonder?" Clark Canton looked where Garry pointed. "In that field?"

"Yup."

"May I go over to see it?"

"I s'pose."

"Thanks." He traipsed away with the cameraman following.

Garry returned to his porch and sat in his rocking chair to watch.

The reporter came back twenty minutes later.

"That's pretty cool," Clark Canton said, wiping the sweat off his forehead. "When did you first notice it?"

"Three days ago."

"Really? Three days? Why didn't you report it?"

" 'Twasn't nothin' unusual."

"They've happened before?"

"Yup."

Clark Canton sputtered. "How often?"

"Ever' so often."

Clark Canton nodded, an uncertain look on his face. "What do you think it means?"

"Stay away."

Clark Canton's eyes darted around. He glanced over his shoulder. "Um, okay then. Thanks." He scampered back to the news van.

Clark Canton's story aired on the *Courier* website, and the gawkers started arriving a day later. In front of his cabin, Garry erected a sign shaped like an arrow pointing toward the field with the words "Crop Circle" scrawled on it. By then, he'd seen no further sign of the Chupe, so he figured it had gotten the message. Having UFO tourists show up to admire his crop circle was a minor inconvenience he could live with.

Until, days later, a rancher discovered a mutilated cow.

Garry saw his neighbor on the local news standing beside the carcass and talking to Clark Canton.

"No way wolves did this," the rancher said, his face stern.

"How can you be sure?" Clark Canton asked.

"Do you see any blood?"

"Uh, no. What does that mean?"

"The blood was sucked out." The camera tracked the rancher as he squatted down and pointed at the carcass. "And look at these incisions. They ain't from animal teeth."

"So, you suspect poachers?"

"What poachers would suck out the blood and then only cut out the heart and liver? It makes no sense." He pointed at the cow's shriveled neck. "See these marks? They ain't natural."

Clark Canton stooped over to view the marks. "Are those taser marks? Or maybe fang marks?"

"You tell me," the rancher said.

Garry knew immediately what they were and what it meant. The Chupe hadn't heeded his warning.

The next morning, Garry rode his ATV across the hills in the direction where he'd seen the Chupian ship. After a short search, burnt and broken vegetation indicated where the ship had landed. A shallow trench carved by the ship terminated against...a boulder? Garry recognized the signs of a holo cloaking device that captured an image of the boulder behind the ship and projected it forward to hide the saucer. It was a rookie mistake to park the ship next to the incriminating evidence.

Garry hailed the ship over the Chupe's normal frequency. On the display his holo provided, the face of a juvenile Chupe appeared. It grimaced when it saw who hailed it.

"What do you want, Gargopuss?" the Chupe asked in the annoying screech of their race.

"Didn't you see my warning? This area is off limits."

"What do I care? It's a free galaxy."

"Some of us are making a peaceful life for ourselves here," Garry said. "Your actions are endangering us. So, why don't you just move along?"

The Chupe responded with the unintelligible squawk they used for laughter. "Kiss my earhole, Gargo. You think Earth is your private playground? Well, it's not. I came here for some nice, juicy beef. I saw it, I took it, and I liked it."

Garry's hair bristled, but he kept his voice reasonable. "You've had your fun. Now go back home before you spoil it for all of us, your race and mine."

It replied with more squawking. "I think I'll stay. I like it here. I might try some elk and bear, too, before I leave."

The transmission cut out. Garry had anticipated the conversation might go this way, so he was prepared. He reached a hand through the cloaking field and stuck a tracker onto the underside of the Chupe's ship. Humans were not as advanced as Chupes and Gargos, but they still produced some clever technology.

A few days later, a beat-up RV showed up at Garry's cabin. A woman in jeans and a ball cap climbed out. She placed her hands at the small of her back as she leaned backward. Garry stepped out onto the porch.

She approached the cabin. "Good afternoon, sir," she said, using her hand to shade her eyes against the sun.

"The crop circle is yonder," said Garry, pointing.

"Thanks. I saw the sign," she said, glancing in the direction he pointed. "I really hoped I could speak with you."

Garry's antennae would've perked up at this, if Gargos had antennae. "Why's that?"

"The crop circle appeared shortly before the cattle mutilation happened. Do you think there's a connection?"

Gargos found it difficult to lie, but when asked a direct question, they could equivocate. "Maybe."

She nodded and gazed again in the direction of the crop circle field. She turned back. "Do you mind if I sit down on your porch to get out of the sun?"

Garry was surprised—and intrigued. Why was she actually here? Maybe he could get her to talk. He nodded his assent.

She stepped up and took Garry's rocking chair, which annoyed him a bit, but he had to admit she looked natural sitting in it. Like it was meant for her. He pulled over a peach crate and perched on it.

"My name is Judy. What's yours?"

"Garry."

"Do you have something cold to drink, Garry?" she asked. "Your high-altitude sun is stronger than I'm used to."

Everything inside his cabin was cold, the way he liked it. If a drink would make her comfortable enough to talk, he could accommodate her.

He went inside and returned with a glass of water.

She took it with a smile. He felt a twinge of satisfaction as she showed him her teeth. It meant he pleased her.

"You've got a beautiful view," she said as she surveyed the valley spread out before his porch. Aspen leaves shimmered in the light breeze. "I can understand why you built your cabin here."

"Yup," he said. "What's your interest in a dead cow?"

She tipped the glass and took a long drink before answering. "Can I be honest with you?"

Why would she ask him that? Garry stared at her without answering.

She nodded as if he did. "I'm an alien hunter."

If Garry had a gorge, he would've gulped. "You think an alien created the crop circle?"

"No. Crop circles are fake," she said. "I think an alien mutilated your neighbor's cow, and I'm here to prove it."

Garry fumed inside. He figured that Chupe kid would be trouble. But this? Fortunately, his holo could only duplicate the deadpan delivery of movie cowboys, so the face it projected never reflected his emotions. It didn't stop the shiver of anger from fluttering the clothes he wore. He placed his hands on the thighs of his jeans to hide it.

"How's that?" His holo voice betrayed no anger and minimal curiosity.

"I saw the pictures." Her eyes bored into him. "The fang marks in the cow's neck, the carcass devoid of blood, the heart and liver removed—all are signs of vampirism."

What could she possibly know? "You believe in vampires?"

"Vampires have existed for thousands of years. The ancient Babylonians told stories of Lilitu, who sucked the blood of babies. The *estries* of Jewish folklore were female vampires. The *striges* of Greek folklore were vampire owls. The Old Norse told of their *draugrs* and the Icelanders of their *draugar*. They existed centuries before vampires appeared in Transylvania."

The Chupes had been coming to Earth about that long. They covered their tracks, but it was inevitable a human would eventually put all the clues together. And now, innocent Gargos like Garry would be caught in the crossfire.

"And you think vampires are aliens?" Garry asked.

"That's what I'm here to prove, yes."

"Some would say that's crazy."

She laughed. Her laughter was a delightful melody, unlike the Chupe's braying.

"You're not the first to tell me that," she said.

"Why come to me, then?"

"I'm gathering data. I want to talk to the people in the area to find out what they've seen. Maybe I can pinpoint where the alien built his nest."

"So, you think it's an owl-vampire alien?"

She giggled. "I don't know. What do you think?"

He had an idea. "Maybe."

She lifted an eyebrow. "Do you know something, Garry?"

If he orchestrated it right, she could be the way to rid himself of that Chupe. "Nothing about vampires. But maybe something about aliens."

"Tell me."

"The crop circle, for one thing."

"You really think an alien did that?"

"Maybe."

"Hmph," she said. "Okay, what else?"

"The night before, I think I saw his ship," Garry said.

She narrowed her eyes. "What did you see?"

"Like a meteor, but different. It landed beyond those hills. I rode over and found signs where it landed."

"What signs?"

"A trench bordered by broken and burnt vegetation."

"You mean a crater?"

"No. Not a crater."

Judy put a hand to her mouth. Excitement glittered in her eyes. She cleared her throat before speaking. "Can you take me there?"

Garry shook his head. "I don't want to spook it."

"What are you thinking?"

"It already hit the Reynolds ranch. Its hunting ground has been discovered, so it won't return there again. The only other cattle herd near here is the Gomez place. He grazes his cattle in the high pasture."

"Can you give me directions?"

"I'll take you there," Garry said. "We'll stake it out together."

The pleasant odor of pine sap filled Garry's breathing tubes as his electric ATV hummed over the carpet of pine needles. As they climbed the hills that led to the cattle's grazing grounds, the cooling air of the deepening dusk reminded him of summer back home. There, temperatures rose above freezing infrequently, and snow was an ever-present joy. Gargos had evolved an antifreeze component in their blood to adapt to that climate, unlike the Chupes, who lived in the equatorial regions of their shared planet. In the resource-scarce polar regions, each Gargo required an extensive habitat, which explained their reclusive temperament. Over time, the polar icecaps had shrunk, squeezing the Gargo population into ever smaller areas. Gargos like him had come to Earth seeking cold climes and open spaces.

Seated behind him on the four-wheeler, Judy rode with her modified Super Soaker strapped to her back. On her head, she wore a helmet with night vision goggles ready to pull down over her eyes. Judy's arms pressed against his middle as she shifted her weight forward to speak where she thought his ear hole was.

"Why are you doing this?"

What should he say—that he wanted a sassy teenager to get off his lawn? "I'm fine with an alien tourist coming for a visit, but when it starts killing the livestock, I draw the line."

"So, you believe in aliens?"

"I believe what my eyes and ears and nose tell me," he replied. "Speaking of which, what've you got in your squirt gun back there?"

She chuckled. "It's garlic juice. A couple of Costco-size bottle's worth."

"What do you plan to do with it?"

"Vampires hate garlic. If he comes for me, he'll get a face full."

"Isn't that a myth? That vampires hate garlic?"

"It's more like a common element of vampire folklore that appears across time and cultures."

"Are you also carrying a stake to put through its heart?"

She snorted. "No, I'm more of a catch-and-release hunter. I'll take a few pictures, then spray him with garlic so he'll be shunned by his family and friends until the stench wears off. Maybe that'll be a warning to others of his ilk."

Garry liked that idea. He liked it very much. "Why not hit him with a tranquilizer dart and tag his ear? That way you can track him wherever he goes."

Judy laughed. "I like the way you think, Garry, but there are gotchas. Would a dart penetrate this alien's hide? What type of tranquilizer would work without killing him? How long would he sleep before he woke up and sucked our blood?"

"Good point," he said.

The ATV left the forest and entered a high meadow. Under the light of a full moon, a breeze created ghostly waves in the grass. Garry steered for higher ground where they could locate the herd. At the top of a rise, the dark silhouettes of cattle appeared in a hollow below. He drove to a position in the shadow of the adjacent forest where they could park and monitor the herd without being seen.

Judy dismounted the ATV, unshouldered her weapon, and stretched her back. She noticed Garry looking at her. "I stiffen up after sitting for a time without adequate lumbar support," she said. "It's a drawback of my age and avocation." She took a seat, facing the herd, with her back against one of the ATV's tires.

Garry sat beside her. He studied her Super Soaker. He'd seen them advertised but never examined one up close. This one looked different from those on the webcasts. Two reservoirs perched side-by-side atop the gun barrel, each the size of a two-liter bottle. Filled with garlic juice, they had to weigh ten pounds. No wonder her back hurt. On television, the kids pumped air into the reservoir like a pump-action shotgun, but this one lacked such a mechanism. "What's that at the rear of your gun?"

"It's a battery-powered air pump." She flicked a switch, and the pump hummed. A gauge showed how much air pressure was set to expel the liquid in the two reservoir tanks when the trigger released it. "Under pressure, it's got a range of thirty meters."

Just the weapon the modern vampire hunter required. And another example of advanced human technology. "You really think garlic juice will be effective against this alien?"

"I'm sure of it."

"Why?"

"I told you: vampires hate the stuff."

"But what if the alien is actually a werewolf?"

"Is that why we're out here tonight under a full moon?" She giggled. "Because you think the alien's a werewolf?"

"Why not?" Garry answered. "Wolves attack cows around here all the time."

"Come on, Garry, be serious. Werewolves don't exist." She grinned.

"They're not any more farfetched than vampires."

Judy's smile faded, and she fell silent. Garry instantly regretted his remark.

"Look, Garry." Judy spoke slowly. "I know what people think when I tell them I hunt alien vampires. That's why I don't reveal it to many people. But they don't know what I know."

"Like what?"

"Like what autopsies of previous cattle mutilations have shown. They detected sedatives and anticoagulants in the cow's blood."

"What do you think that means?"

"It means the mutilations are not the work of natural predators," she said. "The sedatives detected are not naturally produced—at least not on this planet."

"So, where do they come from?"

"Some say human poachers. I say aliens."

"Alien vampires."

"Right. Because human poachers don't suck cow's blood. And human vampires only exist in books and movies."

He followed her twisted logic, but he couldn't believe that theory had led her to this meadow with him on this night.

A map lit up on the display inside his holo. The tracker signal showed the Chupe's saucer was moving, approaching from the south. He trained his vision on the horizon across the meadow. Two minutes later, it appeared. He raised an arm and pointed. "There it is."

In the distance, moonlight glinted off the metallic skin of the flying saucer. Judy inhaled a sudden breath and grabbed his arm. She flipped down her night vision goggles for a better view.

Garry tracked the vehicle as it floated over the sleeping herd. It hovered for a moment above a cow separated from the rest. The craft drifted onward and descended beyond a ridge.

They sat in the shadows of the trees staring at the spot where it disappeared. Their patience was rewarded.

A creature the size and shape of a large wolf edged over the crest and halted. From this distance, Garry found it difficult to make out any details besides its silhouette. It stood in a crouch on its hind legs with its pronounced snout pointing toward the cow and front arms dangling from hunched shoulders. The spikes along its backbone were a clear indication it wasn't a wolf.

"It's a chupacabra," Judy murmured as she viewed it through her goggles.

His holo offered Garry a translation. "Chupacabra" was a Spanish word meaning "goat sucker." But Garry shivered in recognition of its similarity to "Chupe." It couldn't be a coincidence.

As they watched, the Chupe crept toward the sleeping cow. Judy stood and lifted the Super Soaker into her arms. "Once it bites the cow, the chupacabra will be immobilized as it sucks out the blood."

How could she possibly know that? From her vast knowledge of vampire folklore? But how much of that lore was reliable?

Suddenly, the Chupe raced forward and leapt upon the cow. Its arms encircled the cow's head as its jaws clamped onto the bovine's neck. No noise reached them as the cow's body twisted and squirmed. In seconds, the struggle ceased, and the cow collapsed.

Judy set out running in a commando crouch, her gun ready to shoot. Garry hesitated for an instant, undecided what his role was in this encounter. The Chupe wouldn't take kindly to her disturbing it during its kill. It would almost certainly react violently. Garry decided to follow along.

Ahead, the merged form of the Chupe atop the cow remained motionless. Every second brought Judy closer to the Chupe, but the grass deadened the sound of her rapid footfalls. As Garry approached, the moonlight began to reveal more details. The Chupe's hand wrapped around the nose of the cow. Its three-toed feet grasped the cow in a firm grip. Something boxy interrupted the smooth line of the Chupe's skull. Faint sucking sounds reached Garry's earholes.

Judy was twenty meters away when the sucking halted abruptly. The Chupe raised its head—and looked in their direction. The box on its head flashed a blinding light.

Garry's holo blanked out, but not before it absorbed enough light to prevent him from being dazzled. Judy had fallen in a heap. Her weapon and night vision goggles lay scattered a few feet from her body. The Chupe rose up and started for her. Moonlight gleamed off the claws of its outstretched hands.

Garry had no doubt what the Chupe intended. He roared and sprinted headlong to protect Judy.

The Chupe's eyes flashed red in the moonlight as it zeroed in on Garry. When it recognized who was coming, it opened its jaws to expose the fangs it used to subdue its victims. From that open maw, the screech of Chupe laughter exploded. The Chupe halted and braced itself to receive Garry's charge.

That gave Garry the time he needed. He sidestepped past Judy and scooped up her weapon. Slipping his finger through the trigger guard, he rotated the barrel toward the Chupe. Shrieking its rage, the Chupe charged with claws extended and fangs exposed. Garry pulled the trigger.

The stream caught the Chupe first in its chest and then in its open mouth as its feet dug in to avoid the onslaught. The Chupe's scream became a gurgle. It recoiled, turning its snout to the side and raising its arms to fend off the garlic juice. Garry kept pressure on the trigger while directing the stream along the Chupe's side and back as it ducked and twisted away.

The Chupe retreated at a run, howling like the werewolf it wasn't. Garry lifted the gun barrel to keep the shower of garlic juice on target as the Chupe fled. The last of the juice sputtered from the reservoirs, and the stream halted. The Chupe disappeared over the rise. Seconds later, the saucer rose into the sky and swooped off at high speed.

Behind him, Judy began to stir. Garry knelt beside her. She rolled onto her back, and her eyes fluttered open. Her nose twitched. In a drowsy voice, she said, "It smells like an Italian restaurant around here."

She sat up and looked over her shoulder. The cow was staggering to its feet, lowing pitifully. "What happened to the chupacabra?"

"Your gun worked," said Garry. "I sprayed it with garlic juice, and it took off."

She peered at him. "It looks like you got injured." She raised a hand to his face. "Are you okay?"

Although his voice audio still worked, Garry had forgotten his holo display generator had burned out. She was staring at his real face. He stood and turned away. He ducked his head, took off his Stetson, and unfurled the veil tucked into its sweatband. He reseated the hat on his head with the veil covering his face.

"It's all right, Garry," Judy said softly. "I know what you are."

Garry remained mute. What would she do with the knowledge?

"I've seen *The Elephant Man*. I understand now why you chose to live out here all alone."

The next morning, Garry sat on his porch watching the sunrise paint the valley below in orange hues. He'd repaired the holo unit in his Stetson, so he wore his normal face. The door of the RV opened, and Judy stepped out with a coffee cup in her hand. She zipped her jacket up to her chin against the early-morning chill. When she got to the porch, Garry offered her the rocking chair.

She took a sip of coffee. "You don't need to wear your mask on my account."

"Thanks, Judy, but I'm more comfortable with it on."

She nodded. "I understand."

Garry changed the subject. "I don't think your alien will be coming back."

"I don't think so, either." She smiled mischievously. "I dissolved sugar in the garlic juice to make it extra sticky. He'll have a devil of a time getting it off."

Garry activated the chuckle routine in his holo.

Judy reached out and placed her hand on his glove. "Thanks for being there for me last night."

A rush of pleasure swept through his body. "You're welcome." He gave her hand a pat. "If you want to stay here a while, I'd enjoy the company."

"It'll be cold and snowy here soon."

"That's the best time of the year in Colorado."

She laughed. "I'm more of a warm weather girl."

Light unfurled backward across the valley below as the sun rose higher above the far rim.

"Besides," she said, "the chupacabra may be gone from here, but it's likely to surface elsewhere to mutilate some other poor cow."

Garry nodded. She was probably right. He reached into a pocket of his jeans and pulled out a business card. "Here, take this with you."

"What's this?" She squinted at the small print.

"I stuck a tracker on its ship before it took off. That's the information you need to log in and monitor its location—if it's ever within range of a cell tower."

She gazed at him. "You really are amazing, Garry," she said, shaking her head.

"I'll tell you a secret," he said. "Garry is a nickname. It's short for Gargoyle."

Judy tittered. "The right person could truly love you, you know."

Garry detected the warmth in her voice. "That's not in my nature. I came here because I like living alone."

"I know why you live alone. But what counts is not how you look. It's what you have here." She pointed at her chest.

Garry's heart was located in his pelvic area, but he got her meaning.

She finished her coffee and stood. "I'd best be on my way."

He stood with her. "I'm sorry you didn't get any pictures of your chupacabra. Maybe next time."

"What makes you think I didn't get any pictures? I was wearing a bodycam." She stepped off the porch. "I'll send you a few."

Damn. These humans and their weird technology.

With a wave, she mounted the cab of her RV and drove off.

As the plume of dust trailing her vehicle disappeared beyond the ridge, a thought occurred to him. Did her bodycam catch his face as he knelt over her in the meadow?

Hopefully, the full moon backlit his head and nothing registered. But with human technology, you never could tell.

He would just have to trust her to keep his secret.

# About the Author

John M. Campbell grew up reading science fiction and loved imagining a future extrapolated from what is now known. Inspiration for his stories often comes from the strange realities of quantum physics and cosmology. He is a first-place winner of the Writers of the Future contest, and his story appears in Volume 37 of their annual anthology. He joined other Writers of the Future winners to found Calendar of Fools publishing. He has a story in their Kickstarter-funded anthology, *Inner Workings*, along with an essay that reveals how he constructed the story. Other stories of his appear in the online magazine *Compelling Science Fiction* (Issue 12), in the *Corporate Cthulhu* anthology (Pickman's Press), and in the *Triangulation: Energy* anthology (Parsec Ink). For a complete list of his publications, visit his website at JohnMCampbell.com.

John lives and writes in Denver, Colorado.

# Down in the Pit
## by
## Damien Mckeating

# Down in the Pit

## September 1985

**V**iolence was coming. Charlie Burns could feel it creeping over his flesh: an invisible oil slick that suffocated him. His chest felt tight, and his skin crawled with goosebumps.

He stood in a crowd that was hundreds strong, maybe over a thousand. The flying picket had arrived at the colliery, determined to stop the workers from crossing the line. There had never been the same support for the strikes in the Midlands like there had been elsewhere, but maybe their numbers today could shut the pit down.

Charlie looked across the way and saw the assembled police force. As many officers gathered there as miners on strike, he reckoned. Other pickets had ended in violence, and he was certain that was how this one was going.

"Good turn out," said John Barrows next to him. John was a big man, given to slow but even-handed thoughts. Now his brow was furrowed under his beanie hat as he stared at the police.

"Stronger together," Charlie replied with forced cheerfulness. He believed it, absolutely. The union was only as strong as its members, but today… He shivered. Today it felt bloody wrong.

"How can they stomach it?" John asked, nodding toward the police. "Ain't they working men? Don't we all deserve to work and get paid?" He clenched and unclenched his fists, a gesture that didn't go unnoticed by Charlie.

"Keep it steady, big man," Charlie said with a slap on the shoulder for John. It was like hitting a wall.

The crowd started to swell and move. There were vehicles arriving. Men walking toward the colliery. The workers were starting to arrive, and the picket was getting into motion.

"Scabs!"

"Rats!"

Cries went up all around him. Charlie bumped and wavered with the energy of the picket. It surged forward, blocking the road, and Charlie saw the police respond in kind.

"This is getting out of hand," Charlie said. "Somebody's got to calm this down before it turns into a right bloody mess."

John turned to him. There was a flash of blue in his eyes, a sort of electrical crackle that stopped Charlie in his tracks. It was the only animation he could see in John's face. The man looked blank, except for that tiny spark.

"Don't mind a mess," John said.

"Don't sound like you, John," Charlie protested.

His words were lost. The picket carried him along. It met the police line and the two sides clashed, a ripple spreading out along the line of contact.

"Calm it down!" Charlie yelled. "Get back!"

He could see other faces like his, men caught up in the current and being washed along. Here and there he saw it again: that blue spark. A sudden flash of energy in the expressionless faces of men he called friend. Men he'd shared a pint with.

Screams. Yelling. The crunch of flesh and bone meeting in ways they shouldn't.

Charlie stumbled and tried to fight his way back. He shoved and clawed, took a blow to the head, staggered, dropped to one knee.

For a moment there was peace. His ear throbbed and everything sounded like it was underwater. He had no idea what had hit him. There was space around him, a little bit of calm. Beyond it, men screamed, shouted, swore. The police were among them now. Bottles were thrown. Batons came down. Flesh thudded into riot shields.

"Right bloody mess," Charlie said. He put a hand to his face but there was no blood.

He tried to stand but the mass of bodies barrelled him down. He lay on the ground and shouted. It was hot. There was heat rising up through the mud and grass. He jolted up, looking for burns on his hands. It was like he'd touched a pan on the stove. How his hands weren't blistered he didn't know. Even now he could feel the heat through the knees of his jeans.

Charlie looked up, searching for answers, and saw John come crashing down. There was blood on his face. His lip was split. Looked like a tooth was missing. A mounted police officer came barging after him.

Charlie screamed. The horse pressed forward, a massive weight, a stomping threat of hooves and muscle. The officer riding it looked down and took a swipe with his baton.

Charlie raised his arms to protect himself.

The pain turned his vision black.

He remembered screaming.

And not much else.

It was an austere office. Grey walls. A flat-pack desk and chairs. It was a spare room that was getting ideas above its station. A clock hung above the door. The second hand didn't tick, it turned in a seamless stream of movement. Charlie hated it. He liked the tick-tock of the mechanism at work.

Charlie sat at the desk. His broken arm was in a cast and strapped up for support. He cradled it to his chest. He had wrangled himself into his winter jacket, and his wife had helped make sure his hat was on straight.

On his left sat Jack Wright, a man who seemed to have been born embedded in the mines and unions. His face showed the price of it; creased with worry and crumbling under gravity. On Charlie's right was Bill Jones, a young man with a furrowed brow and an unpleasant tension rippling through his muscular frame.

Across from them sat a man and a woman. The man was angular, thin, dressed in a suit and tie. The woman was prim and proper, bolt upright in her chair. A thin scar ran in a line around her throat. The savagery of it pulled at Charlie's gaze. It looked out of place on her.

"Thank you for coming, gentlemen," said the thin man. "My name is Arthur Jenkins. This is Naomi Smith. I can't stress enough the importance of what we have to discuss here today."

"You're not National Coal Board," said Jack in his mine-deep voice. "I know all of those bastards, and you ain't one of them."

The NCM were the government body responsible for closing down the mines, for breaking the pickets, for selling to the public the economic unfeasibility of continuing the coal industry.

"No," Arthur said. "I'm from the Department for Oversight."

"Oversight of what?" Jack asked.

"Everything," Arthur replied with a tight-lipped smile.

"So, what have we got to discuss?" snapped Bill. He jabbed at the table with a finger, driving his words home.

"Quite simply: the coal mines must close," said Arthur.

The two men to his left and right laughed. Charlie stayed silent and thoughtful. He'd been a union man for a long time. He was used to the bluff and bluster of government men. Something in Arthur's tone unsettled him. It was too…matter-of-fact. As if Arthur was announcing something he had already seen happen.

"You can't do it," Bill insisted. "Those are our jobs. Our lives. Don't you understand? Look at you, never done a day's work in your life."

"You're destroying families," Jack added. "Destroying communities."

Arthur interlocked his fingers, resting his hands on the table. "Weighing the needs of the few against the needs of the many," he said. "Communities." He held out a hand as if weighing an invisible object. "Against the country." He held out his other hand, suggesting a balancing of scales.

"What are you talking about?" Bill shook his head. He gestured at Naomi. "Have you got nothing to say for yourself?"

Charlie winced. It would benefit them all if Bill's few brain cells could fire up quicker than his mouth on occasion. Naomi just fixed him with a cool stare, her blue eyes unwavering. Charlie stared at those blue orbs and remembered the flash of light in John's eyes. He remembered the heat coming through the ground.

"Mrs Smith is here as a special consultant," Arthur said. "Alas, a previous accident prevents her from expressing her opinions vocally with us today."

Bill sat back in his chair, his frown giving way to a moment of embarrassment.

"What does Thatcher think she's doing?" Jack asked. "Coal is a British industry."

"The Prime Minister is well-aware of the situation. Indeed, her background in chemistry and x-ray crystallography have made her better suited to this crisis than any previous leader of government."

"Crisis?" Jack scoffed. "What crisis?"

"There's something in the mines and it's dangerous," Charlie said.

Arthur gave another tight smile and nodded at him.

The weight of the words silenced Jack and Bill. They realised what had already become apparent to Charlie: this was about more than economic policy.

"What is it?" asked Bill. His bluster was gone, his voice soft.

Arthur opened up a briefcase and put a photograph on the table. It was a large, clear image, but it still took a moment for them to understand what they were seeing.

"A crystal?" said Jack.

Against a background of dark stone was a blue crystal. It grew from the rock. It was the translucent blue of a summer sky, and all three men gazed into its angles and geometry and felt themselves drawn deeper and deeper into the refracting lines and patterns of its beautiful, unyielding construction.

Arthur turned the photograph over and the spell was broken.

"It's worth money, then," Bill declared.

"It's alive," said Arthur.

Charlie shivered. He heard the other men scoff, but he could feel the truth of it. Even in a photograph the stone felt wrong.

"Like a fungus," said Arthur. "They may appear on the surface miles apart, but under the ground they are one organism. This blue stone infects the British Isles."

"Stone can't be alive," Jack said.

Charlie shook his head. Why had Arthur had to use the word infect?

"I can show you," Arthur said. "When you have witnessed the threat to our country, the deal is this: support us in shutting down the mines. What's below the earth must remain undisturbed."

Charlie couldn't help but feel like a traitor as they went into the mine. He wasn't crossing the picket line, he wasn't going to work, but just going into the mine at all felt wrong.

The mine itself, deep in Yorkshire, was shut down. There was no one to see what they were up to. The five of them had travelled in silence, Arthur driving them in a black car with tinted windows. He went round the winding country lanes with a speed even Charlie, born and bred to such roads, found reckless. In the solitude of the journey, Charlie found himself re-assessing the two government officials.

They opened padlocked gates. Went down concrete hallways. Through metal doors. Along walkways with yellow railings, paint flecked and dirty. They switched out their winter coats for high-vis jackets and safety helmets. Charlie winced as he negotiated his broken arm.

Arthur hung up his suit jacket and rolled up his shirt sleeves. Charlie saw marks and tattoos down the man's arms, spiralling symbols etched and carved into the skin.

"Department of Oversight?" Charlie asked.

Arthur gave one of his tight smiles, revealing nothing. "Whatever the work requires," he said, and popped a safety helmet onto his head.

Charlie looked over at Naomi. She was ready, the safety gear clashing enormously with her long skirt and blouse. She had a silk scarf around her neck, hiding the scar. Charlie noticed for the first time that she was wearing heavy boots, like a rocker or punk.

Noticing his attention, she fixed him with a steady stare. The blue of her eyes flashed, or had he imagined it?

Charlie looked away. She unnerved him. So silent. So observant. Sometimes she seemed to turn, listening, hearing something they couldn't.

"Let's get this over with," Jack said.

"Nonsense," Bill added with a shake of his head.

Time and the journey had allowed scepticism to creep in. But Charlie had a coldness in his stomach. A terror he had never felt in the mines before.

As the other men left the room, Charlie found himself alone with Arthur and Naomi.

"Do I want to see what's down there?" Charlie asked.

Arthur looked at Naomi, as if the two of them were sharing a private conversation. "No," he said.

The five of them reached the lift and down they went.

The mechanism clanked and rattled. Slow and steady they wound their way down into the earth. The headlamps on their helmets lit up patches of rock as the metal cage descended. Charlie had been in the mines when his light failed. It was a darkness like nothing else. Your eyes played tricks on you. It was too dark; your brain had to make things up just for something to do.

The temperature rose as they fell. No air moved down in the mine. It was humid and hot. Sweat sprang up on their foreheads, trickled down past their temples. Arthur wiped at his face with a handkerchief and Bill scoffed.

"Aye, it's real work down here," the young man said.

"Never doubted it," Arthur replied.

Half a mile below the surface, the lift jerked to a stop. It opened onto an underground platform: a functional area of concrete and metal safety bars. A train waited for them, open metal carriages with four seats in each. The three union men climbed into one, the two government officials in another.

The train lurched into life.

Another hour would take them to the coalface.

The rattle of the train was harsh, clacking from the metal rails bouncing off the stone walls. The three men sat with their heads down, huddled together.

"You ever hear anything like it?" Jack asked.

"They're hiding something," Bill insisted.

"Whatever is it, we take it to the press. Get them on our side. Show people what's going on. How dangerous can it be?"

"Might be radioactive."

"And we're down here without safety gear?" Jack shook his head. "Those two wouldn't go anywhere if there was a risk of breaking a fingernail."

The two men laughed.

"Let's see," Charlie said. "You ever heard about the Department of Oversight? Because I haven't. I think those two have seen more than they're letting on. Can't you feel it? Something creeping over your skin?" Charlie held up his hand, but there was nothing to see.

"That's just the heat," Jack said. "Always been sweaty in the pit."

"Getting scared of the dark?" Bill joked.

Charlie sat back. He listened to the steady click-clack of the rails, and the play of his headlamp over the support struts as they flashed by in the darkness. Half a mile down, tons of earth above them, undiscovered country below them. Miners always said the pit was like an alien environment. Now, more than ever, Charlie felt the truth of it.

The train rocked to a halt.

"We're not there yet," Jack called. "Coalface is still a way off."

"We're where we're going," said Arthur. He turned, his headlamp illuminating a side passage off from the rails.

"What the hell is that?" Bill asked.

The opening was jagged and rough. Like a tear in the earth.

"We don't know," Arthur replied. "We didn't dig it."

And he led them into the darkness.

They went in silence. The heat stole their breath. Sweat ran down their faces, down their backs, pooled under their arms. Charlie had never heard the mine so quiet. No roar of machines. No camaraderie, jokes, or stories.

Charlie wiped at his hands and arms. He felt suffocated, beyond the heat and sweat. He was used to those. Something he couldn't see was clinging to him, crawling over his flesh. He wanted to tear into his cast and scratch at his arm.

"We're nearly there," said Arthur. He laid a reassuring hand on Charlie's shoulder. "Look."

"What is that?" Bill asked.

Ahead of them there was a blue glow. It diffused in the air like a fog. An ephemeral swirl of colour, like bright dust particles. A few more steps and they emerged into a cavern.

The blue crystals, like in the photograph, grew out of the walls. Out of the ground. Out of the ceiling. Their glow revealed the vastness of the space. It was a cathedral. A holy site. They moved with hushed steps. They felt a presence shift its awareness to them. Their own attentions were pulled to a long, slender spine of crystal that descended from the ceiling and almost reached the floor.

Jack wiped at his eyes. Tears were streaming down his face. "What is it?" he asked. "What's going on?" He sobbed and sniffled.

Bill shuffled toward it, hand outstretched, fingers tentatively close to that slender blue spine. "What does it want?" His voice was awed.

"We don't know," Arthur said softly. "What we do know, is that we would like it to stay asleep."

Charlie saw a flicker in the crystal's light, an ebb and flow in the energy that took him back to the picket line. "We have to leave," he said, turning to Arthur. "I saw it. I saw it in John's eyes. That blue spark."

"There's power here," said Bill. A spark of energy jumped from the crystal to him. His eyes flashed.

"We can't stay here," Charlie argued.

"Naomi," Arthur said, a warning in his voice.

Charlie felt/heard a keening in the air. It was a sensation that defied his senses. There was music, he could feel it, but the sound was a piercing whistle that scraped along his bones.

Bill bellowed and charged. The big lad rammed into Jack and slammed him against a wall of crystal shards. They pierced his flesh, leaving Jack impaled on the wall. Slivers of blue grew out of his torso and face. There was no blood, and Charlie thought maybe the walls were drinking it.

Bill turned to them. His eyes blazed blue.

Arthur grabbed Charlie and pulled him back. Charlie stumbled. The world tilted. He struggled to raise his foot over a step while his eyes insisted he was on flat ground. He needed to hold onto something as the cathedral tilted. As a compromise he fell to his knees.

Naomi and Arthur stood between him and Bill. The world was twisted forty-five degrees. He didn't understand how anyone was standing up.

Bill opened his mouth and the sensation-sound changed. It rippled under Charlie's skin and made his broken arm throb.

Naomi started to glow. Her fingernails glittered like blue shards. The veins under her skin radiated blue light. Her eyes lit up like jewels, and her hair crackled with electric sparks. Her own sound-sensation, that vibration, slid around the room. It undulated, came in waves, a gentle ocean of non-sound that Charlie felt in his insides.

It was a lullaby, he realised.

Naomi was singing it to sleep.

Like a fractious baby, the crystal entity resisted.

Charlie closed his eyes. A wave of nausea rocked his stomach. His brain assured him he was falling, turning over and over in empty space, although he could feel the hard stone underneath his fingers.

In the darkness behind his eyes Charlie saw lines of light. They sparked from a single point on the horizon and flew toward him. In a heartbeat they broke, refracted, formed patterns more complex than he could follow. His brain raced for context: the pattern of his veins; the flow of rivers; the growth of trees. Each a mirror on a mirror, a pattern on a pattern. All the same and all different.

Charlie cried. He could taste his tears, and it made him happier than he had ever been. The sensation of water, the taste of salt, tied him back to the world.

"Up you get," Arthur said. He hooked an arm around Charlie and dragged him to his feet. "Let's get some fresh air."

Charlie stumbled. He looked back. The cavern-cathedral was darker. Something had closed its eyes. For now.

And there...a shadow in the dimming blue... It had to be Bill. His skin pieced by jagged lines. Turned into a silhouette of a ragged man. Unmoving. Unfeeling.

Naomi followed them. There was a blue spark in her eyes. Her skin was rich with the colour of it, a living body of ocean.

The journey to the surface was a dream for Charlie. In his sleep he remembered shaking and crying, but in his waking hours it was difficult for him to bring to mind. In the end, he realised, his only conscious memories were based on his dreams, which in turn were based on... He didn't know.

Eventually there was sunlight on his face. It was weak, late autumn sunlight, but it felt warm and life-giving all the same.

"It's alive," Charlie said, confirming it to himself as much as anything.

"It is," said Arthur. He sat down next to Charlie on the grass bank overlooking the mine. He still had his coat off and shirt sleeves up, showing off the tattoos and scars.

"What is it?"

"Something that fell from space," Arthur shrugged. "Way before evolution even had the idea for the dinosaurs. Something from the beginning."

Charlie shook his head. He wanted to ask what it wanted but could see the futility of the question. There was no understanding to be found. There was no commonality, no human desire or motivation that could be attached to it.

He looked over to where Naomi stood. She had her back to them, the wind whipping at her coat and hair. There was no trace of blue to her now.

"She sang it back to sleep," Charlie said.

"This isn't our first turn on the merry-go-round," Arthur winked.

They sat. Charlie sniffled, wiped at the dried tears and snot on his face. His arm hurt like hell, and he cradled it against his chest. "I could tell people," he said.

"Go ahead," Arthur waved a hand, gesturing at the expanse of open countryside in front of them.

He'd be branded a madman, of course. Charlie could see the tabloid headlines now. It would ruin him. It would ruin his family. "You brought us here to die."

"No," Arthur said emphatically. "I brought you here to show you. Some are more sensitive than others. Didn't expect Bill to go the way he did. You're sensitive too, but with some natural resistance. Could have a use for you."

"No. Thank you." Charlie risked another question. "Where is Bill?"

Arthur shrugged again. "Physically, he's down there. Part of the mine now. Part of it. Mentally, spiritually…who knows?"

"What now?" Charlie asked.

"Help us to get the unions in line," Arthur said. "The mines will shut down. The industry will be gutted. Communities will collapse. Families will plunge into poverty. But an alien intelligence, whose motivations we can barely conceive of, will remain asleep."

"Jesus," Charlie sighed, thinking numbly that his old schoolteacher would have clipped him around the ear for blaspheming.

"Come on," Arthur said as he stood up. "I'll give you a lift back. There's a nice greasy spoon just in town. Bacon, sausage, beans, and chips sound good about now. Mug of tea with a whole bunch of sugars in it." Arthur smiled, but this one was genuine. "And then back to work."

He turned and walked away, leaving Charlie to catch up.

Just like that.

As if nothing had even happened.

# About the Author

Damien is a UK writer with a lifelong love of fantasy and the supernatural. Childhood days were spent reading, writing, playing tabletop roleplaying games, engaging with the popular ball-related sports of the day, and trying to communicate with the dead. He would eventually set aside necromancy and sports and go on to study film and writing at university. After a stint as a copywriter for radio, he moved into SEN teaching.

Over the years, he has had short stories published across different magazines and anthologies, both for adults and children. He has also written for comics and radio, and the peculiar folk band Hornswaggle. He's fond of corvids and is currently the oldest he's ever been. Sometimes he remembers to blog about writing at skeletonbutler.wordpress.com. His debut novel, Tallulah Belle, is a supernatural coming of age story set within the walls of a fantasy burlesque theatre and is due for release in 2024.

# Just Add Salt
by
**Al Simmons**

# Just Add Salt

**H**ave you ever seen the classic sci-fi film, *Invasion of the Body Snatchers?* I'll bet you didn't know it was based on an actual story that took place in Alameda County, right here in the Bay Area where I live. They say the film is getting another remake, only this time they plan to tell the true story.

In the film, the aliens seeded the Earth with pods that dropped from the skies and assumed human form to become non-sentimental, carefree semi-humans, or a hybrid human/alien mix.

In real life, they arrived much earlier, decades, in fact. It was a modest showering. The first hybrid groups mixed well and shared technology. Industrial revolution, anyone? They were peaceful, practiced non-violence, followed the law, stayed out of trouble and the news, and life went on. They called themselves Alterians because they altered their appearance to resemble the native populations, to blend in, wherever they went.

The Alterians were basically intelligent seeds, a thinking man's seed pod.

They came out in the late 1950s, with the advent and popularity of sci-fi movies. Though fiercely competitive but with nothing to compete for on Earth. Perhaps that wasn't the case on other planets. The real reason the Alterians got along so well with humans had less to do with their peaceful nature and willingness to share advanced scientific benefits and technologies, and more with genetics and the existential threat removed once they realized digesting the other was impossible, due to their lack of sufficient matching genetic markers. For Alterians, carbon-based life forms based on DNA formatting were as nourishing as sand is to us. Pod people grew their own food supplies.

Alterians and their descendants were self-sufficient and contained within their pods ample food stores to sustain them for a limited time, plus a seed library should they reach a land rich in the cadmium required for their unique bio-systems to thrive. Their cell structure required cadmium to grow just like DNA-based life systems required nitrogen-rich soil to flourish. The Alterians wandered the galaxy on a limited resource platform, living a strict scientific existence, only procreating when necessary to maintain their numbers.

Straight interspecies cross-pollination didn't work with humans and Alterians, despite the physical similarities and familiar mammalian pleasure feedback reward mechanisms inviting many to try. Alterians were easy to find attractive since they tried so hard to resemble you. But, if you wanted to successfully mate with an Alterian, you had to go the pod route and give up your humanity first.

To me, personally, Alterians were like hybrid corn: all starch and no story. Up close, they even smelled like high-fructose corn syrup. I admit, I invited one home more than a couple of times. She was addictively attractive. She even tasted just like high-fructose corn syrup. But, in the end, I had to cut her off like a bad habit.

The whole idea of dating an alien was insane. Nobody liked her. She was rather dry. But the inability to procreate was the underlining issue.

"A nice human girl isn't good enough for you?" my mother argued, accusing me of near bestiality.

But once they let themselves be known to humans, life on Earth changed for the Alterians. They should have kept to themselves. The federal government got involved and dedicated a piece of land in Utah to the Alterians, rich in cadmium and not much else, to establish a reservation there, and to get them out of the general population, who had grown uneasy with the idea of aliens among us, and giving new meaning to unalienable rights.

The official government land grant made it clear the land had the cadmium requirements the Alterians needed, though not enough cadmium to support an alien population explosion. There was enough cadmium to sustain their numbers, and maybe a little more.

So, that's where the lot of them went off to, the first Alterian Reservation on Earth, in central Utah, about 100 miles west of the Great Salt Flats.

The relocation turned out to be a total disaster for the Alterians. Who knew salt would affect them that way? On their second night on the reservation, they held an outdoor meeting and were stargazing beneath a spectacular clear desert sky when a sandstorm downwind from the Great Salt Flats caught them by surprise and lit them up like sparklers on the 4th of July, turning them a deep emerald glow, and within seconds they were all burned to a crisp.

Leave it to the dogs to discover salted aliens, cooked right, were digestible.

But, here's the thing, according to chefs associated with the Salt Lake City Gazette, once prepared, salted, and cooked, the Alterians tasted just like BBQ chicken: juicy, and kind of sweet. Bad news for the few remaining Alterians, because once the news got out, they never stood a chance.

Even today, tossing salt over your shoulder is still required, pre-entry, at some big-city, high-end conservative venues.

# About the Author

Al Simmons was twice recipient of Illinois Arts Council Awards, Poet-in-Residence, City of Chicago, 1979–80, and Founder of the WPA, World Poetry Association, and The Main Event, World Heavyweight Championship Poetry Fights, Chicago, Illinois—Taos, New Mexico, 1979–2001. He has been quoted on the front page of the *New York Times* Living Arts Section. He was nominated for a 2021 Rhysling Award. His work has recently appeared in 43 magazines and anthologies since 2017, including *Abyss & Apex*, *Kanstellation*, *Urban Arts*, *Illumen*, *The Novelette-Dark Fantasy*, *The Reckoning*, *Path of Absolute Power*, Dyskami Press, *Cosmic Horror Monthly*, *Cutleaf*, and *Punk Monk*. He lives in Alameda, California.

# Make Earth Great Again!
by
L.N. Hunter

# Make Earth Great Again!

D r. Gah-Reg tapped twice on the star chart with his primary manipulatory tentacle. "System D77F9 looks promising. The third planet sits in the habitable zone, nicely obscured by a handful of gaseous giants further out."

"And the chemical makeup of the planet?" asked Councilor Del-Han, sucking heavily on a sulphur-infused stogie.

"Not so encouraging. The surface is heavy on carbon, lower order metals and some trace elements. However, the atmosphere is weaker than we require, saturated with nitrogen and oxygen. While it shouldn't be too expensive to add more carbon and sulphur dioxides, there is the complication of an infestation of indigenous life."

"Intelligence rating?" Del-Han asked, looking toward his chief xenobiologist, Professor Clan-Tett.

Clan-Tett cleared her fore-throat. "Most of the lifeforms, about seventy percent, are at or below level one, flora, bacteria and the like. Twenty percent level two, insectoid. Another eight percent are level three, avian, reptilian and mammalian, but with limited consciousness. The remainder, Lord Councilor, are level four—intelligent, technically able, but relatively uncultured, as demonstrated by the existence of something they call 'reality television.' With a population of the order of seven billion, they could be problematic."

"Level four you say... Hmpf. Space flight capability?"

"They've left the planet a few times but haven't progressed beyond their major satellite to any significant degree. My guess, it'll be a few centuries before they manage to reach farther than the limits of their solar system. They're rather fragile monkey derivatives and currently incapable of withstanding the rigors of interstellar travel."

Del-Han rubbed his under-chin. "Anyone else know about them?"

"No, sir. There has been no previous analysis of this sector; we're the first vessel to spot them, and we haven't yet filed the Intelligent Species Discovery report."

"Delete the ISD. We'll obliterate the planet's life. No one will be any the wiser."

"Councilor!" Professor Clan-Tett waved all five manipulators in agitation.

"Grow an exoskeleton, Clan-Tett," Del-Han growled. "They're centuries away from level five—you said so yourself—and we have our own problems. Why should we care about a lifeform that doesn't contribute to the galactic economy?"

The occupants of Clan-Tett's armada had been forced to leave their planet due to lack of habitable space and the resources to live, and none of their neighbors would accept them as refugees.

Gah-Reg broke the ensuing silence with a cough. "If I may offer a suggestion."

The others looked at him expectantly.

"As you know, Your Honor, my expertise is in terraforming, and it is indeed a costly task, more expensive than we can sustain without seeking assistance in this instance. I wonder if we could encourage the planet dwellers to do it for us. You know, trick them into converting their atmospheres to something we would find more comfortable, without us spending more than a pittance. And if they do it to themselves," Gah-Reg shrugged, "we're merely taking advantage of their mistakes."

"Why in Great Ash-Lonn's name would they trash their planet for our benefit?" bellowed Del-Han, employing both back and fore lungs to emphasize his displeasure.

Gah-Reg smiled, letting his war tusks show. "The planet's wealth distribution is very non-uniform, and all we need to do is give the have-nots a chance to take their share."

Clan-Tett muttered, "It'll never work," but was ignored by the others.

Two men met in a village within a small rain-forested region in the African sub-continent, so small it didn't have a name of its own.

"Colonel Bakr, as a sign of our faith—no, our *belief*—in your right to rule this land, we offer you these weapons." Carrick strode along the row of crates his men had dragged off their lorry. He flicked the lids open, one at a time: "Rocket propelled grenades…land mines… mortars…and, of course, the ever-popular AK-47."

Nazim Bakr, one of several warlords in the area, eyed Carrick and his men suspiciously. "Why are you doing this? What do you want from us?"

Carrick spread his arms wide and laughed. "Nothing, my dear Colonel, nothing at all. They're yours to keep, and to use as you see fit." He tapped a finger against his chin as though something suddenly struck him. "Perhaps, when you're victorious, we might be permitted to return, for further conversation, yes?"

Bakr nodded absently, his attention fully occupied with thoughts of his new toys.

Bakr didn't notice Carrick visiting three other warlords in the area. But then, how could he? The visits all took place at the exact same time, but it was the same Mr. Carrick, with the same battered ex-US army truck, and the same two sullen, burly helpers carrying identical crates of weaponry.

Job done, the four Carricks and their entourages drove out of sight of the villages and teleported back to their ship now in orbit around Jupiter.

"Ugh, that place stinks. And this skin, it's disgusting." One of the Carricks, Officer Krunk-Daq, complained, peeling the mottled, hairy latex disguise off his naturally purple epidermis. He sucked heavily on a sulphur dioxide cannister, restoring his chemical balance after several hours breathing Earth's atmosphere.

Councilor Del-Han snorted. "Get used to it, soldier. If this is a success, you'll be going on many more missions like that."

Within days, Bakr launched attacks on Karundi and Balaatu outposts, but was surprised at their resistance. The three armies were evenly matched and decimated the rain-forest before their leaders realized that their fleeting victories were not improving the situation of their dwindling populations.

This time only two Carricks came visiting.

"Colonel Bakr, I see you are not doing so well."

The haggard-looking warrior growled, "Someone has been arming my rivals. We need more weapons."

"My dear Bakr, we would be privileged to assist you." Carrick nodded at his truck. "But, before we hand over the merchandise, there is something we would like you to consider. You lack ambition."

Bakr growled wordlessly.

"Calm yourself, Colonel. I merely mean that you are aiming your sights too low. If you defeat the Karundi and Balaatu, what does that gain you? Control over a few hundred square miles. Who will notice, who will know the name of Bakr?"

Carrick spread his arms wide. "What if you ruled the country? Your government is weak. Weak and corrupt. You could be president and bring wealth and status to many more people. You could have a seat with the world's leaders. Make peace with your Karundi and Balaatu brethren, and attack your capital."

At the same time, the other Carrick was meeting with President Yawanda and his chiefs of staff.

"President, it pains me to see the turmoil in your fine country. Your work over the past five years is being undone by ungrateful rebels. Don't they know what's best for their own people?"

He spread his arms wide. "What if you could squash them once and for all? Imagine, peace throughout the country, and influence with world leaders. I am not alone in believing in the future of your country—consider us a group who wants to do what's best. For a start, we would like to offer you these weapons…"

"Well, Dr. Gah-Reg, how is your exercise progressing?"

"I think you'll like what you see, Your Honor." Gah-Reg projected photographs and maps onto the screen in front of them. "As predicted, Bakr is laying siege on the capital, and the warfare is spreading to neighboring regions. Look here: the data indicates rising levels of carbon dioxide, along with sulphur and nitrogen oxides, as the result of fires and many, many decaying corpses."

"Excellent," Del-Han said, as he stroked the aloof-looking white bolo-lizard on his lap.

Clan-Tett squinted at the figures. "Excuse me, sirs, I'm only a mere xenobiologist, but there's something I don't quite understand in the data. Might I ask a question?"

Councilor Del-Han extended his head spines, annoyed at the interruption but grunted assent.

"While the esteemed Doctor's chart shows an increase in these nourishing compounds, it is over a very small area and during a very short time interval. If I may?" She reached over and grabbed the slide clicker from Gah-Reg and projected one of her own charts. "This is what we see if we double both the area and the timescale: almost negligible increases in these chemicals, and even those tail off after a few planetary rotations." She placed the clicker on the table with a satisfied and somewhat smug clack.

Gah-Reg's eyes, all of them, bulged as Del-Han glared at him, head spines fully deployed and pulsating. He stammered, "Lord Councilor, it was only a small-scale experiment. We merely need to give them larger weapons."

"Ash-Lonn's sticky pellets!" said Clan-Tett, dropping her pretense of humble lack of understanding. "My charts clearly show diminishing returns as we invest further. These monkey-men have had nuclear weapon capabilities for many of their solar cycles; they've even dropped atomic bombs on cities, in a country called Jah-Pahn. Yet still, they return to peace. Warmongering alone is not the answer."

Councilor Del-Han directed his glare at her. "What's your suggestion, Professor?"

Professor Clan-Tett returned his stare. "Despite the small brains and having only two manipulators, they've managed to develop a world-wide communications network. However, they've not been smart enough to make it secure; they think they control their creation, but they can't definitively establish the veracity of anything on their interwebnet." She snirpled in amusement. "Of course, most of them do not realize this."

She paused with a look of uncertainty, breathing spiracles flashing orange and green. "I beg your forgiveness, Lord Councilor, but I have already carried out an experiment of my own."

"I'll deal with your breach of protocol later," growled Del-Han. "But, continue for the moment."

"I've developed a concept I call 'fake news'…"

In the bowels of the spaceship, Professor Clan-Tett's communications specialists had been exploring the interwebnet, injecting packets of information and then monitoring how quickly and how far they propagated. The scientists were particularly intrigued at how the messages morphed into distorted copies of themselves.

A series of dispatches outlining the imminent demise of several rare level two and three species in Austraal-Ya proved to have a very short lifetime. On the other hand, news about the reproductive habits of one of the Kardash-Yan clan circled the planet several times before being extinguished only by the appearance of a new boy band, though Clan-Tett couldn't establish precisely what one of those was.

Clan-Tett watched as her chief cyber-specialist, Intelligencer Ray-Nat, formulated two separate message packets: one listing a number of naturally occurring foodstuffs and their benefits to the level fours, and the other listing the same foods and how they hastened death. Receiving a nod of approval from the Professor, he pressed a key and launched both messages into the planet's communications network.

After a moment, Rey-Nat blurted, "Professor, look!"

Clan-Tett stared at the screen, her entire scalp wrinkling in concentration: "That can't be right. One should be pulling ahead of the other; they can't be equal."

"Look closer. They're even being 'licked' and 'finger-upped' by the same individuals. It's as if they don't think for themselves."

"Maybe foodstuffs aren't sufficiently important to the level fours, and we should use something more significant. What was that you said about one of the bigger countries electing a new leader? What if we injected messages on that topic? Imply that one leader is anti-environment and the other pro."

Rey-Nat taps at the keyboard again, manipulators almost blurring as he typed.

A few moments silence again, then Clan-Tett hisses, "Oh, pellets of immense stickiness. How can he be winning? Quick, add some more: golden showers, underhand dealings, consorting with the country's enemies, anything to slow him down."

"Nothing's working. What do we do now, Professor?"

Clan-Tett rubbed her chins. "Let's try something so ludicrous they can't possibly believe it. Start transmitting ridiculous statements on their 'Twitterings' as if coming from this one, so that his followers will turn away."

"And that's how we got to here. We accidentally caused Uss-Ya to elect a small-minded clown as their king, though he turns out to be a perfect leader for our purposes.

"Regard his head spines. Bright yellow and standing proud, just like yours, Your Honor. It must be an omen. But we must rely on more than omens! Look at this graph."

She reached for the clicker and showed the air quality and temperature data over North America. "Here we have the worst weather, the worst pollution, and the most extreme variations in temperature this continent has ever experienced, overtaking our experimental control countries, Chine-Ya and Ind-Ya. While you were," she sneered at Gah-Reg, "playing soldiers in Affrik-Ya, I was making Uss-Ya practically habitable for us.

"I've already got some ideas for other suitable leaders, to accelerate the increase of pollution on the planet's other continents." She clicked forward to a slide showing another human with similarly attractive head spines. "Oh, don't be fooled by this one despite its similarity with Uss-Ya's king. It's called a Borr-Iss from a small country called Yoo-Kay. I'm not actually sure if Borr-Iss is a level four. The country seems to be an offshoot of Uss-Ya, and this Borr-Iss may be the Yoo-Kayans' attempt to show respect to Uss-Ya by cloning their leader, which would explain the strange behavior of this creation. The place is a lot less important than its current occupants seem to think.

"When they're not protesting in favor of or against their leaders, the monkeys are too busy with their 'slebritty gossip' to care what happens to their planet, to *our* planet."

Del-Han smiled for the first time that day and rubbed his manipulators together. "Well done, Professor. We'll give the Urth the leaders they want, and they'll give us the world we want."

# About the Author

L.N. Hunter's comic fantasy novel, *The Feather and the Lamp* (published by Three Ravens Publishing at the end of 2022), sits alongside works in anthologies such as *Best of British Science Fiction 2022* and *Hidden Villains: Arise*, among others, as well as several issues of Short Édition's *Short Circuit* and the *Horrifying Tales of Wonder* podcast. There have also been papers in the IEEE *Transactions on Neural Networks*, which are probably somewhat less relevant and definitely less entertaining. When not writing, L.N. occasionally masquerades as a software developer or can be found unwinding in a disorganised home in Carlisle, UK, along with two cats and a soulmate.

Publications list: https://linktr.ee/l.n.hunter

Facebook: https://www.facebook.com/L.N.Hunter.writer

# The Texas Pteranodons

by

Z. M. Renick

# The Texas Pteranodons

I t was the middle of January, 1976, when teenagers near the Texas-Mexico border reported seeing a creature that looked like a giant bat, a bat as tall as they were.

It was late February, in San Antonio, that three elementary school teachers saw the same thing: a black creature with wings like a bat that stretched for nearly twenty feet and a skeleton that seemed to stand out beneath the wings, casting an enormous shadow over the road on which they were driving. It was a creature all of them, teenagers and teachers alike, said looked exactly like a pterodactyl.

It wasn't until the first week of March that anyone thought to call me about this.

George Middleton was in charge of the San Antonio branch office of the agency I work for, an agency that doesn't appear in any federal government directory. He was clearly old school. The sixties and early seventies had passed without affecting his fashion sense in the slightest; he was wearing a grey suit that would not have been out of place twenty years earlier. I approached his desk warily; such men often had issues working with women. However, when he saw me, he just smiled and said, "Ah, Miss Ballentine. You look just like the picture by your column. Thank you for coming so quickly."

That's me. Leah Ballentine, gossip columnist extraordinaire. Blond-haired, blue-eyed, and empty-skulled. If it involves a famous man cheating on his wife, or a beautiful actress being a slut, I'm there with all the details. If it involves anything more weighty than that, I'm not interested. Or so I've convinced everyone to believe.

Middleton asked, "Have you read the briefing?"

I nodded. "Dinosaurs near the border, huh?"

"Of course, they aren't dinosaurs, but the question is, what are they? Too many people have seen them—too many sensible and reliable people—for them to have been simply a figment of some kook's imagination."

I considered the problem. "Ornithopters, perhaps." No one had ever succeeded in making a mechanical bird that could fly like the real thing, but that didn't mean someone hadn't done so now. "A mutant, maybe?" All kinds of strange creatures had crawled out of the desert after the Trinity tests, though none this dramatic. "Or, of course, it could always be aliens."

"Your job is to find out which, if any of those, it is. We've interviewed all of the named witnesses, but we've also figured out, based on the timing, that there were a number of other people in the area at the time." He handed me a list. "None of those people will talk to an official agent, and our unofficial agents haven't gotten them to admit to seeing anything. Those upstairs think that you can do better."

I scanned the list. "Any particular information you want from them?"

"As accurate a description as you can get. Any details, no matter how small. And what direction the creatures went. We'd like to trace them back to their point of origin."

"Consider it done."

Middleton looked skeptical. "You're quite confident."

"With reason. I'll let you know what I find."

I left Middleton's office and looked down the list along with the pictures beside each name. *Katie Linden, 16, believed to have been at her boyfriend's house that morning and would have needed to return home along that road. Joseph Thompson, 71, usually walks along that route in the morning. Emily Simon, 27, another teacher at the school, lives in the same area as the others, should have seen the same thing.* There were a few other names on the list, in decreasing probability of having been in the right place to see anything. Those three, however, seemed by far the most likely to have information. I planned to start with them. First on the list, and in my thoughts, was Katie Linden. Teenagers, especially teenage girls, were child's play for me to manipulate.

The last thing I wanted was to have some sort of official interview. I needed to talk to Katie somewhere she would be relaxed, somewhere she wouldn't be busy, and most importantly, somewhere where her parents wouldn't be present. The mall seemed like a good bet. School was on the verge of getting out, and if Katie was like most teenagers, she'd be in a hurry to get there and do nothing as soon as the final bell rang.

By the time I got to the mall, the halls were full of kids. I scanned the various cliques but didn't see anyone who looked like Katie. In the food court, however, I got lucky; I walked in just as a boy and a girl were coming in through the outside doors—and the girl was Katie! I wasn't thrilled about trying to talk to her with her boyfriend hovering over her, but fortunately, they separated at the doorway, and the boy wandered off somewhere in the mall while Katie went to join a group of giggling girls sitting around a table drinking sodas. Perfect.

I went to get myself a lemonade from the Hot-Diggity Dog stand and carried my tray over toward the girls. They were annoyingly absorbed in their own business, so I kicked a chair as I walked by. As expected, the chair banged into a couple of others, creating a racket, and causing everyone in the food court to look my way. *Mission accomplished.* As I made my way over to a table right next to the girls, I could hear the whispers starting up. I sat down, and I was able to hear enough to make out the words.

"That's her! I'm sure it's her!"

"You're seeing things. I mean, yeah, it kinda looks like her…"

"It's totally her! See the way her hair curls under her neck? And that little mole by her ear? That is totally Leah Ballentine."

I decided this had gone on long enough. I turned around and smiled. "Are my ears burning?"

The girls all gaped at me. The one who'd been speaking stopped and just stared with her mouth open. Another sputtered, "Uh… Ah… Are… Um, that is… Are you Leah Ballentine?"

"Well, I was born into the Ballentine family, and 'Leah' is what my mother called me, so I guess I am."

"Wow, this is so cool," one of the other girls said, in a voice barely above a whisper.

Throughout all of this, I had been keeping my eye on Katie. She wasn't one of those who had said anything so far, but she was gazing at me with a look I recognized as starstruck. I smiled again and indicated an empty seat at their table. "Do you mind if I join you?"

The girls scurried to make room for me. They all introduced themselves, and I committed their names to memory. The one sitting next to me, Tiffany, asked, "So, what are you doing in San Antonio?"

I looked around the room, then said in a low voice, "I'm working on a story about David Cassidy." I met each girl's eyes as if inviting her to join my conspiracy.

"David Cassidy is here? In San Antonio?" Katie squeaked. It was the first time she had spoken. It appeared I had made the right choice in celebrity.

"See, I *told* you that that was David Cassidy I saw near the park the other day," said another girl, named Nancy.

"No, it wasn't," Tiffany said. "It didn't look anything like him."

I leaned in closer. "Tell me what you saw. Whether it was or wasn't him, it's worth hearing. I can confirm it later!"

Nancy told me a tale of a young man, who almost certainly wasn't David Cassidy, buying an ice cream cone, and then one of the others chimed in with a story of that same man making out with a girl behind the restrooms. Another girl claimed that, no, it wasn't *a* girl, but a set of identical twins he'd been making out with. The stories grew more and more lurid with each iteration. I took out my notepad and started jotting stuff down, vowing to burn these pages as soon as I got home; I was pretty sure that if word of them ever got back to Mr. Cassidy, he'd be in my office screaming about libel (technically something must be published before it becomes libel, but many actors failed to appreciate that fine distinction). Nonetheless, I encouraged the girls to keep talking. When they ran out of material about the supposed appearance of David Cassidy, they moved on to other celebrities and celebrity lookalikes. I listened as carefully as I could, putting my "that is the most fascinating thing I've ever heard" expression on my face for every single one of them. Heck, I still had a gossip column to file this week, and some of this stuff might even be true.

At last, the stories wound down. I sighed. "I guess I ought to be going to do some further investigation. Unless anyone has anything else…"

The girls looked at one another. Then, one of them said, "Katie had something weird happen to her the other day."

"It wasn't the other day," Katie said quickly. "It was a while ago. And it's not the sort of thing Miss Ballentine wants to hear about."

I picked up my pencil. "Tell me. Is there a scandal? Does it involve anyone famous?"

"No, no. It's nothing like that."

"Oh." I affected disappointment. "Tell me anyway. I might not be able to use it in my column, but I bet I know someone else who can."

"It's really nothing…"

"Come on, tell me. I'll keep your name out of it, if you want, but I'd really like to know." I leaned toward her. "Some of my best stories come from listening to people like you. I'd love to hear what you have to say."

As I had suspected, being the focus of attention of a celebrity was having an effect on Katie. Would she tell what she knew, if it meant keeping that attention? I was willing to bet that she would. I was right.

"It was last week, I guess. Last Wednesday... No, Tuesday! That's right. I remember, because Keith and I were watching *All in the Family* the night before. At any rate I was sneak—er...coming home that morning, and I was kind of lost in thought, when suddenly I looked up, and there was this *thing* standing right in front of me."

"What kind of thing?"

"I don't know. I thought it was a bird at first. It had a big beak and those beady eyes. But then it opened its mouth, and it had *teeth*. I wanted to scream, but I was too scared. It was so close I could feel it breathing on me. It smelled dusty, like those old trails that my parents used to make me go hiking on. And kind of nasty too, like the stuff the janitor uses. It opened its wings. It was huge; it seemed wider than the road. But there were no feathers, just skin. It took off and flew away."

I nodded. "Did you see which way it went?"

"North. Toward the center of town." Katie suddenly looked scared. "Please don't tell anyone I told you that. My parents would *kill* me if they knew I'd spent the night at Keith's."

I promised. I spent a bit more time with the girls, signing a few autographs, before I graciously excused myself to ponder what I'd learned. It wasn't much. Katie's description clearly suggested that the creature was biological, which would eliminate ornithopters as a possibility, but other than that, and a vague direction, I had no more than I did when I began.

I considered the next name on my list, Joe Thompson. A man in his seventies would be a very different challenge from a teenage girl. I couldn't count on him being wowed by a famous gossip columnist or stories of celebrities. But there were still ways. Once people get to a certain age, they usually have things that they want to complain about. If I could figure out what Joe Thompson's was, convince him I was writing an article on it, and he could vent to me... That would get me in the door, and once I was there, I'd find a way to ask him if he'd seen the supposed pterodactyl. It would require being flexible and thinking on my feet, but I had a reputation to maintain, and I'd find a way to do it.

I made my way to the Thompson farm and knocked on the door of a yellow farmhouse. A white-haired woman in a light blue dress answered the door. "Yes, how can I help—" Her voice suddenly stopped, and her jaw was left hanging open.

I wasn't sure if this was a good thing or not. "Good afternoon. My name is Leah Ballentine. I'm a reporter. I was hoping to see Joe Thompson…"

"He's busy," the woman said, still staring at me as though *I* were the pterodactyl who had appeared sixty-five million years away from the proper time. "He's with Leah Ballentine. In the living room. He's…with you!"

"What?" All sense of decorum gone, I pushed past the woman into the house. She seemed too stunned to resist.

Beyond the door was a sunny, whitewashed hallway. At the end of the hall, I could hear voices. I hurried down there and found myself in an old-fashioned parlor. There was a piano in one corner and six plush chairs scattered about the room. Two of those chairs were occupied. One was facing away from me, so I could only see a white head sticking up above the red velvet back. The other, however, was facing the door, and I could see the blonde woman occupying it. It was…me!

The man with his back to me was talking, but I didn't register any of the words as I just stared at my double. Eventually, she looked up and saw me, and her eyes got as wide as I imagined that mine were. The man must have seen her reaction, because he stopped talking and turned around to see what she saw. His eyes grew wide as well. "What the—" he started to say.

The three of us stared at each other for what seemed like ages. At last, my doppelganger broke the silence. "Well, this is awkward."

She jumped out of her chair and ran toward me. As she did so, her body shifted. Her face grew longer as her skin turned a pale green color. Her legs became as skinny as sticks. She scurried past me, and her dress—a dress that had turned into a wrap the same green color as her skin was becoming—brushed against me. It felt leathery but delicate, almost like vellum. Then, she was past.

"Hey, don't you dare!" I shouted.

"Who the hell are you, lady?" Joe Thompson yelled. "What the hell are you?"

We both took off running after the mysterious figure. Thompson leaped up and started moving faster than I would have thought possible. By the time the creature reached the front door, both of us were in hot pursuit. The old woman, whom I assumed was Thompson's wife, wisely stepped out of the way. We reached the front door, took the porch steps two at a time, and chased the creature across the fields.

As soon as the creature made it out of the house and into the open fields, it opened up the wrap, which turned out to be wings. It spread those wings, caught the air, and started to glide. Despite the situation, I caught my breath. I was seeing what hadn't been seen for millions of years: a pterodactyl in flight. I knew it wasn't a real dinosaur, but it still was enough to capture the imagination of my inner child. And yes, I have an inner child. I'm not a complete cynic.

But no matter how cool it was, I wasn't about to stop chasing the "pterodactyl." It had impersonated me, and it was going to pay for it.

Thompson might have been an athlete in his youth; certainly, he was in far better shape than I would have guessed based on his age. But his knees had been around since Teddy Roosevelt was president, and eventually, that started to show. He stumbled, winced, and started to fall behind. But I kept going. Trying to chase down a flying lizard might be an exercise in futility, but I was going to try as long as I could.

Only…the lizard wasn't really flying. It was gliding, yes, but it never seemed to go any higher than about eye level, and then it would slowly drift to the ground and start running again. Slowly, I *was* gaining on it. I was now so close that I could reach out and touch it. I made a flying leap and tackled the pterodactyl.

I struck the creature near its shoulders, and it gave a pitiful squawk as delicate bones broke under my weight. I winced in sympathy, sorry to have caused harm, but having caught the shapeshifting alien masquerading as a dinosaur, I wasn't about to let it go.

The creature writhed under my grasp, but I held on fast. The bony wings became arms again, and the long beak collapsed into a human face. Soon, I was staring at myself again.

The other me said, "Let me go!"

"Not a chance. Not until you tell me who you are, what species you're from, and why you've been running around Texas disguised as a dinosaur."

"I haven't been… That is… Ow!" She winced, and I realized that I'd been holding tightly to her shoulders. They didn't feel broken—I guess her shapeshifting had healed whatever damage I'd done to the bones—but they still might be sore from what I did. I shifted my grip to her upper arms, but I didn't loosen it.

"I wasn't running around disguised as a dinosaur. I took that form… Well, I was surprised when I saw you, that's all. I hadn't expected our paths to cross so quickly. And having you catch me looking like you, I… I just wanted to shift into something else. I took the first form that came to mind—the pteranodon, just because I've been thinking about it constantly for the past few days."

"But why were you talking to Joe Thompson while disguised as me?"

"Same reason you wanted to talk to him, I imagine. Figuring out what he knew about the pteranodon."

"But you—" I shook my head. Talking to myself like this was just too weird. "If you really are a shapeshifter, do you think you could look like someone else?"

"I will if you let me go."

"If I do, will you just run away again?"

"I won't. I promise."

I didn't know if I should trust that promise, but my arms were getting tired. I didn't know how much longer I'd be able to hold her anyway. The promise was better than anything I'd get if I just waited until she managed to slip away. I let her up, and she shifted again. This time, it wasn't nearly as dramatic as her shift into the pterodactyl: her hair changed to white, her features moved slightly, and her skin acquired wrinkles. Soon, she looked like Joe Thompson's wife. That was still a little weird, but I decided it was a level of weird that I could deal with.

The woman pushed her way to a sitting position, and I sat down beside her. The two of us must have been quite a sight, sitting there in the muddy fields. But my outfit was already a mess based on what I'd done so far, and getting a little more dirt on me seemed a fair trade for some decent information.

"So, let's start again," I said. "Who are you?"

"My name is—" She let out a series of squawks that seemed they would be more appropriate coming out of the pterodactyl she had been than the human whose appearance she was assuming.

I winced. "I don't think I can pronounce that. Does it translate?"

"On my planet, in the language of the Iceborn, it means roughly, 'the first light of a newborn star.'"

"So, er, Dawn? Can I call you Dawn?"

She seemed amused. "That will do. As to what species I'm from, well, our name for ourselves would probably be just as useless to you as my name was, but we've interacted with your government before, and I believe they refer to us as Species Sigma-Alpha-Three-Two-Six."

I shrugged; the designation meant nothing to me. One of the unfortunate aspects of the government agency I work for is that they have a "need to know only" policy, and they're not very good at guessing who needs to know what. "So that just leaves the question of why you're running around disguised as a pterodactyl."

"A pteranodon," she corrected me. "Pterodactyls are much smaller. And, as I told you, I'm not."

"People have seen you—"

"I know they've seen the pteranodon, but they haven't seen *me*. Other than just now, I haven't taken pteranodon form in at least five years."

"Okay, then, why others of your kind are—"

"They're not." She held up a hand. "Just let me explain. As you've probably guessed, my people are shapeshifters. Over the eons, we've expanded our powers by collecting biological specimens from a thousand worlds. A few dozen million years ago, by your reckoning, we came to this one and collected some of the species that you call dinosaurs. The pteranodon has always been a creature of particular interest for us. You see, we've always wanted to fly."

"But you're shapeshifters? Can't you shift into birds and stuff?"

"We can shift our *shape* into birds, but those annoying laws of physics still apply to us. We can't change our mass, and the various flying animals that we've found have all been much lighter than us. We haven't been able to scale up the principles that let them fly to let us do so. The pteranodon, however, is big enough that, we hoped, we'd be able to get around that. But it hasn't worked out that way. We've mastered the shift into pteranodon form, but we haven't yet figured out how to fly. The studies on the mechanics of what the creature does have been slow. Recently, someone suggested that we might learn more if we watched the pteranodons on their native world."

"Why? Can they not fly on your world?"

"No, they can."

"But, if they can fly on your world, and if your world is really where you want to fly…"

Dawn sighed. "Look, it doesn't make sense to me either. But those were the orders we got from the bosses. They rarely make any sense."

"Bureaucrats. I understand."

"That's one species that seems to be the same on every world we visit," Dawn agreed. "So, we obeyed, we brought the pteranodons to what we thought was an uninhabited bit of desert, but... Well, habitation has moved a bit since the last time we were on this planet...and mistakes were made...and the upshot is that a couple of the pteranodons escaped. My job is to get them back. I was looking for clues as to where they might be when you walked in and...you know the rest."

I still had one question. "If you were shifting into the pteranodons, why did you turn green?"

Dawn looked at me like I was an idiot. "Because pteranodons *are* green."

"No, they're not. They're black."

"No. I've been working with these creatures for longer than you've been alive. They're green."

"But all of the witnesses I've talked to have described them as black."

Dawn paused. "I never thought to ask. I knew what the witnesses saw. I just needed to figure out what direction the pteranodons went. But...if what they were seeing was black... Could these guys have all seen something else? No, that's too much of a coincidence."

I wondered just how much of Leah Ballentine she had copied when she took on my appearance; Dawn's thoughts were running along the exact same track mine were. "People started seeing things that look like pterodactyls—sorry, pteranodons—at the same time you lost two of them. They must be the same. But they're black... Could they just be dirty?"

"Both of them? Well, maybe. Especially if they were nesting some place that was just covered in soot."

Covered in soot... I remembered Katie's words, about how the creature had smelled: *like the stuff the janitor uses*. Ammonia, maybe, which would suggest some sort of industrial plant. "What about an abandoned factory? Could the pteranodons be nesting in an old smokestack?"

"They could. It would be just like them. Now, if we can only figure out which smokestack."

"One witness told me that the creature headed north."

"Joe Thompson told me the same thing before we were...interrupted. So, we're looking for an abandoned factory, north of here... Hang on." Dawn reached into her pocket and pulled out some kind of device, probably one that would allow her to find old smokestacks to the north of us.

I was way ahead of her. I might not have a magic pocket map, but I had done my homework on the city I was investigating. "There's an old cement factory in town. That seems like a good place to start. Let's go."

"Let's? As in, let *us*?"

I hoped she wasn't going to be difficult. "You stole my identity. The least you can do is let me finish the job I came here to do. Let me give you a ride to the site."

"I—well, okay. I'll have someone meet us there with what we'll need to capture the pteranodons."

We got in the car, and I sped through town as fast as I dared without attracting the attention of the cops; Middleton and the others in my agency could always get me out of a speeding ticket, but the traffic stop would mean a delay that we didn't want.

We drove up to the factory and saw the crumbling walls, the grass and moss growing in the masonry, and the huge, silent smokestacks standing guard over it all. I felt the chill that I always get when I go to abandoned places. I can handle aliens, sasquatches, and mysterious green goo falling from the sky without breaking stride. But places like this, ones that were once bustling and full of life but are no longer, give me the heebie-jeebies.

There was a large truck, a semi, parked next to the factory, and Dawn indicated that I should pull up next to it. Just outside the truck, there was what looked like a giant gecko sitting on top of a ten-foot diameter can of tuna crisscrossed with glowing blue lines. Dawn got out of the car, and the gecko, clearly another member of her species, shifted into a young man.

Dawn asked, "So where's everyone else?"

"There is no one else. It's just me."

"Just—what's everyone else doing? What are they up to that's so much more important than recapturing the pteranodons?"

The man shrugged. "There are two of us, two pteranodons, we should be able to handle it."

"'Should' is such an interesting word," Dawn muttered. "Well, never mind. We've got what we've got. Let's get started and hope nothing goes wrong."

She reached onto the can and pulled off some of the crisscross markings, which I now realized were a net. The man pulled another net off, and Dawn turned to me to explain.

"These nets are powered, and we can snap them closed at command. We put the nets on the ground, then when the pteranodons land on them…" Dawn smiled and snapped her fingers. "There's a current running through the cords, which will keep the pteranodons from tearing them once they're inside."

"And how do you intend to get them inside?" I asked.

"That's what this is for." The other alien tapped the can. "Rigelian flatfish. The pteranodons love it, even more than what they used to eat back when they lived on your world. We've packaged the fish in their own oil, which should make them extra fragrant. We'll scatter this on the nets, and the pteranodons will come."

"You might want to stand back," Dawn warned. "Stay behind your car, at least thirty feet. The pteranodons should be focused on the fish and blind to everything else, but… Well, like I said, stay back."

I wasn't about to disobey. I went to Dawn's suggested position and watched as she and the other alien spread out the nets, then opened the can. Almost the second that they did so, a cry came from the smokestacks. An enormous head, with a long beak coming out of the front, and a huge crest coming out of the back, poked out from one of them. The head turned back and forth, and then, seemingly liking what it sensed, came further out. It slithered from the smokestack, and then with a pop, opened its wings and turned into a great kite, almost big enough to block out the sun.

The first creature was followed by a second, and the two circled the smokestacks a few times before descending on the piles of fish that Dawn and her companion had placed on the nets. Seemingly oblivious to the danger, they started to feed. I saw Dawn step out from behind a tree and make some sort of gesture that I guessed was a signal to her companion. Then, she shouted, and the edges of the net she was standing next to came flying up and locked themselves together. The pteranodon gave a squawk of outrage and flapped its wings furiously, but it only succeeded in entangling itself further. It was trapped.

Dawn turned to me and gave me a smile. I returned it, but then I saw behind her the second pteranodon, bits of net hanging from its beak. I cried, "Look out!"

Dawn dropped to the ground right before the pteranodon bit at the empty air where her head had been. It had to settle for raking its claws across her back. She screamed. I remembered that she had managed to heal herself with her shapeshifting before, but I still worried. The free pteranodon was coming around for another pass, determined to avenge the insult and free its mate.

In my purse, I had a small pistol. I reached in to grab it, then pulled my hand out. My little gun seemed hopelessly inadequate against such a giant monster. But I had to do something! I looked around for another weapon, something capable of taking on a dinosaur. I only saw one thing: my car. I hopped into the driver's seat, turned the keys, and revved the engine.

As the pteranodon swooped down, I sped toward it. My timing was perfect, and just as it was about to make another attack on Dawn, I crashed into it. The pteranodon went flying backward and struck one of the crumbling walls. Several bricks fell onto it, and it stumbled to the ground, clearly in no shape to fly.

Dawn and the other alien had made good use of the time I had bought them. In a moment, she had joined me with yet another net as well as a hovering board that was about two-thirds the size of your average New York apartment. The two of them eased the board under the injured pteranodon and used the net to secure it.

Dawn said something to the other alien in their own language, and he responded in a tone that, if he were human, I would have described as confusion. She said something else, sounding worried, and shifted into the giant gecko form as she scurried off.

I didn't know what to do, so I just waited as Dawn went off and the other alien made soothing noises at the pteranodon. He maneuvered the board into the air and into the back of the semi, where the other pteranodon already waited.

After a couple of minutes, Dawn came back. She went to her fellow, had a brief conversation that seemed to be a disagreement, and then came over to me.

I smiled at her. "Well, it looks like we did it. Your pteranodons are back."

"Yes. Thanks to you, in part. I appreciate it. But there is one slight problem."

I felt the hair stand up on the back of my neck. "Which is?"

"One of the escaped pteranodons was female. And, well, our records say she was ready to lay eggs. This one isn't. Now, it's possible that someone made a mistake. That does happen, more than I'd like to admit. But there are two other possibilities. One is that this is that female, and she already laid the eggs somewhere. I checked, and it wasn't here, but that doesn't mean that she might not have had another nest somewhere else."

I wondered if baby pteranodons, somewhere out in the desert could take care of themselves. But that wasn't what really concerned me. "And the second possibility?"

"Is that someone made a mistake when they said only two pteranodons had escaped. The egg-laying female is still out there somewhere—and possibly others as well."

Two days later, I was back in the San Antonio field office.

I handed Middleton my report containing a full explanation of everything I had seen as well as what had happened to the pteranodons—and Dawn's speculation that there were still more. Middleton accepted it without comment, and I reflected a bit on the irony of the fact that, though I was famous for my writing, the most interesting stories I had to tell would all be filed away somewhere no one would read them.

But that was the price for serving my country—and my species— the way that I did. Meanwhile, I was luckier than most agents in that I did have an outlet if I wanted to be recognized. I put Dawn and her pteranodons out of my head and focused on the column I had due in a few days. I ran through the names of various celebrities in my head, wondering which of them would be the target for Leah Ballentine's next investigation.

# About the Author

Z. M. Renick was born in Boulder, Colorado and spent almost all her life there until she went to Smith College in Northampton, Massachusetts. She returned to Boulder to do her PhD in theoretical computer science, then worked as a postdoctoral researcher in the related field of computational biology. She wrote science fiction and fantasy during the copious free time that a PhD student and scientist usually has. As funding got shorter, however, her free time grew more extensive, and now she's a full-time writer.

Currently, she lives in Longmont with her husband, daughter, and a Labrador retriever the size of a small horse. When she's not serving as the ringmaster of that particular circus, she enjoys hiking, swimming, and playing poker as well as writing. She is the author of numerous short stories as well as The Seelie Court series of urban fantasy novels.

# Virus
## by
## Lyndi Alexander

# Virus

Report from Gov. Ship Saukar, team 17-JRG, star system 49x, 700 cycle-unit.

Commodore Elat, science officer in charge:

A s reported earlier, we have followed the expected trajectory of the enemy to a system with a yellow dwarf star and nine planets. Only one of the planets, the third, has the sort of atmospheric conditions which would appeal to the enemy. We have brought our entire laboratory network to bear, forcing the gene sequence mutation on the dominant species on this planet. While sub-species of mammals show random mutations in line with our objective, none have spread as quickly as intended. As the sub-species are not sentient by our definition, we are simply noting their reaction, but will not include it in our success.

Our charitable work with the dominant species continues to be thwarted by the species itself, as they believe themselves to be intelligent and empowered. They have developed various counteragents to the insertion of the forced gene sequence mutation. These seem to be distributed in relevant proportion to the size and concentration of what appears to be forms of government organization. In areas where there is less political association and less affluence (as evidenced by the availability of food, shelter and personal wealth), we have seen more virus infections, as said population cannot easily obtain said counteragents.

Because this is an extremely social and overcrowded world, we were dismayed to find that once the virus was detected, even before developing the counteragents, the governmental agencies imposed strict bans and curfews to prevent individuals associating with each other in public places. Large public events and venues have been cancelled and closed. This has significantly affected our ability to contaminate them in large segments as previously planned. We hoped to have fully transformed this specific population's gene pool within the next 100 cycle-units, but as we generate new mutations to the virus, they continue to develop further counteragents and other plans to thwart us.

We persevere, brainstorming creative solutions, as our intention remains to alter the balance of the planet's population by way of the infection, which they have named COVID-19. It is now doubtful that we will infect them all in time.

In response to the advance of counteragents, we have modified our active virus for greater transmissibility, releasing the tenth mutation in the current time period (designated on the planet as 2021) with moderate success. It spread across most of the planet's land masses within a very short span. We have more mutations prepared and set to be released if the counteragents and other precautions enforced by the political rulers continue to block the process.

It is unfortunate that some deaths have occurred in the course of inoculating this world. The counteragents have succeeded in ameliorating side effects for those not yet changed by the forced gene mutation, and that is to be commended. As far as we know, the mutation perseveres even in these cases. However, the loss of even a million lives to save the remaining seven billion is a debate for ethicists, not scientists. For now, we must continue to change the gene pattern of every living creature that we are able to affect. Our duty is no less.

It would be much easier if we could communicate directly with the species on this planet, to explain that we do not intend harm, but in fact, seek to protect them against the invasion force that is even now on the verge of their star system. The Vigrat seeding ship has registered on our sensors and will not be farther than 350 cycle units away. By that time, if we succeed, all life on this planet will be poisonous to the Vigrat and they will have to move past to another system to colonize. This planet can avoid what happened to our home world.

But our earliest attempts to interact were met with such violent rejection that we have withdrawn our representatives. All we can do is remain outside their capabilities of detection, follow our objective, and continue to infect the planet's residents, forcing the gene mutation to continue until every last species target has been tainted. This we will do until the Vigrat are able to detect us, then we must move on.

We will, as ordered, report again in 100 cycle-units. Team 17-JRG, signing off.

Report from Gov. Ship Saukar, team 17-JRG, star
system 49x, 870 cycle- unit.
Left Order Officer Sigron, science corps:

Apologies for the delay in sending our report.

The Commodore was killed in an attempt to close down a factory producing the virus counteragents on the planet some 45 units ago. They were quite dismayed at the widespread development of the so-called "vaccines" and traveled to the planet to deal with the issue at its production facilities. None of the soldiers who accompanied them survived the incident, so we have no first-hand account, but certain pictorial representations became available on the planetary computer network. These showed that the Commodore's shape-altering device malfunctioned while in the company of members of the dominant species. As you might imagine, this caused some difficulty with the native population. We believe the Commodore may have destroyed the unit in order to preserve our anonymity.

The second cycle-mark of our attempt to protect the planet draws to a close with varying degrees of success. The political units below continue to diplomatically spar with each other about the reality of the virus and the need for countermeasures. We are fortunate that there is a strong percentage of the population that refuses the vaccines, even in the face of their neighbors and even their leaders becoming infected with the virus. In this segment, the virus has taken hold fairly thoroughly. While the main population has withdrawn from public venues, even holding their young back from educational facilities where they would easily pass the virus among them, these citizens campaign to carry on life as before.

We have no interest in the geopolitical subdivisions of this planet other than their efforts to hamper our mission to protect them from the ravages of the Vigrat. Our sister ships that have gone ahead to the next system in line report a higher success rate, and we envy them. If only we had a more intelligent, or at least a more unified, populace to convince. We have not heard from the ships we left behind at star system 35K for several cycles; we take this to mean the Vigrat found and destroyed them. The Commodore believed they might yet escape. If they have reported in from a new location, we would be grateful to hear news of them.

We have temporarily removed hundreds of randomly-chosen individuals from the planet for testing. Results show that those who have received the counteragents—a growing number each unit-mark—display some indicators of the basic virus matrix within their bodies' cells. Their scientists have designated the mutations we have released by letters from one particular geopolitical subdivision. To date we have gathered reports of the success of four strains: Alpha, Beta, Delta, and Omicron. While we have strained the resources of our laboratory facilities and our dwindling number of researchers to come up with new variants, we have yet to see the percentage of worldwide infections we believe will poison the world for the Vigrat.

Our administrators estimate we will be able to continue the fight for another 100 unit-marks. At that point, either we will have exhausted our supply of viral matter, or the Vigrat will have arrived, and we will be forced to leave the planet. Send orders accordingly. We shall report again in 100 cycle-unit-marks, unless we have received contrary orders in the meantime.

Report from Gov. Ship Saukar, team 17-JRG, star system 49x, 950 cycle-unit.
Cicroy, admin staff understudy:

Reporting in, as per instructions of last science officer. No science personnel remain aboard our craft at this cycle unit to file a report.

Those of us who endure have nearly exhausted our resources, both for the benevolent contamination of the planet and for our own survival. Our ship arrived at this star system having already seeded one planet on our travels, and while we had hoped at that time to proceed onward to rendezvous with friends and family on other escape vessels, it is clear we have come to the end of our mission.

Admin had not been made fully aware of the fanatical drive of the science division to save this single planet's population despite its rejection of our efforts. Perhaps we could have diverted necessary reserves to provide for our own continuation. Instead, we have discovered that Science Division continued to closely monitor the humans' development of each individual counteragent or vaccine and almost vindictively prepared new viral mutations to attack each one. Worldwide, governmental agencies reported 50,000 or more new identified cases of the virus at the beginning of the cycle unit designated 2023, which is a significant slowdown since the first virus was introduced but indicated that new infections were still occurring. Despite this, even minute changes were made, and more strains of the virus spread, at great cost to our ships' stores.

Three star turns ago, one of the younger scientists developed a particularly virulent strain that killed half of the lab staff immediately. Mechanical lockdown prevented those of us on the admin side from instant termination, but we were also unable to help those who survived the first blast and were forced to watch on the internal monitors as they descended into painful oblivion.

A secondary lab facility has been constructed by those admin and janitorial members who wish to continue the mission. Frankly, many are discouraged to the point of lethargy and very little has been accomplished.

It has come to our attention, while preparing this report, that the Vigrat seedship has unexpectedly appeared from behind the planet's lone satellite. We have neither the personnel nor the fuel stores to escape orbit at this time. Hasty conference has led to a consensus that we should attempt to physically block the ship from approaching the planet, contaminated as we are, though it seems to this writer a futile gesture. The Vigrat ship is twice our size, and for all we know, is fully provisioned. But, for better or worse, we have always been a people who allowed the majority to rule, and so the government ship Saukar comes to an end. Advise any who would follow us to pass this system by; this species cannot be helped.

    For the Glory of all.
    Cicroy, signing off.

# About the Author

Lyndi Alexander always dreamed of faraway worlds and interesting alien contacts. She has been a published writer for more than forty years, after working as a pizza maker, a floral designer, a journalist, and a family law attorney. She lives as a post-modern hippie in Asheville, North Carolina, a single mother of her last child of seven, a daughter on the autism spectrum, finding that every day feels a lot like first contact with a new species. She is ruled by three crotchety old cats, and six kittens of various ages.

# From the Editor

I've long been fascinated by Roswell, NM. Did a UFO really crash there in 1947? Were aliens and flying saucers actually recovered? What really happened? Who knows? There are many conflicting stories, and although many people really want to believe we were visited by intelligent beings from elsewhere, there is no proof that actually happened.

But the possibility remains intriguing. I thought it would be fun to do an anthology, the theme of which would be What Really Happened. When I proposed this project to Sam Knight, I thought I'd get stories that were only related to UFOs, or alien sightings. Instead, the writers took "What Really Happened" to heart, and I got a vast variety of stories. They include weird bales of hay, werewolves, the Marie Celeste, computer games, and, oh, yes, aliens and alien encounters.

I want to thank every single writer here. Your stories have been amazing. Thank you.

— Sheila Hartney
December 18, 2023

# Additional Copyright Information